MARSHALL McLUHAN

MODERN MASTERS

Already published

MODERN MASTERS

EDITED BY frank kermode

marshall mcluhan

jonathan miller

NEW YORK | THE VIKING PRESS

Copyright © 1971 by Jonathan Miller
All rights reserved
Published in 1971 in a hardbound and a
paperbound edition by The Viking Press, Inc.
625 Madison Avenue, New York, N.Y. 10022
SBN 670–45876–7 (hardbound)
    670–01912–7 (paperbound)
Library of Congress catalog card number: 71–104150
Printed in U.S.A.

ACKNOWLEDGMENTS

Vanguard Press, Inc.: From *The Mechanical Bride*
by Herbert Marshall McLuhan. Copyright, 1951, by
Herbert Marshall McLuhan. Reprinted by permis-
sion of the Publisher.

CONTENTS

MARSHALL McLUHAN

Introduction

It has sometimes been said that Marshall McLuhan's most impressive achievement is his reputation; but although most people are familiar with his name, and some know his more dramatic mottoes, only a small section of the reading public is directly acquainted with the main body of his characteristic ideas.

In an ironic way, this disproportion between McLuhan's fame and his familiarity is central to the endeavor to which he has committed himself; for the very growth of his own reputation seems to bear out his well-known thesis about the way in which modern knowledge is so widely shared within what he calls the global village.

If, as McLuhan claims, the human community is returning to the condition of tribal oneness, the fact that his own name has become one of the most vivid myths within this extended community is surely an impressive piece of evidence in favor of that theory. I find this particular argument both tendentious and unconvincing, but I must nevertheless acknowledge the astonishing growth of McLuhan's reputation, since it tells us something else about the way in which intellectual prestige is promoted within the network of modern communications.

Although McLuhan has displayed amazing productivity in recent years, the only book upon which any serious claim to our esteem can rest was published and widely reviewed at the beginning of the 1960s. Since then, most of what he has said has been repetition or else a series of witty glosses upon the themes announced in *The Gutenberg Galaxy*. I feel that I can safely introduce his main ideas by summarizing the argument of this book alone, although I recognize that there are striking epigrammatic novelties to be found scattered in almost everything that he has published up to the present time.

In fact it is rather difficult to summarize the sprawling arguments of *The Gutenberg Galaxy*. Not only is the range of its cultural reference wider than anything that can be encompassed by a single critic, but the discussion is organized in strict obedience to the main thesis in a fashion that actually forbids straightforward linear précis. This is no accident on McLuhan's part. He has deliberately laid out the evidence in what he calls a mosaic fashion, placing ideas and quotations side by side in suggestive juxtaposition, leaving the reader to draw his own conclusions as to their mutual significance. In doing this he has unfairly anticipated our consent to his claim that imaginative truth is distorted by explicitly linked arguments.

Since I remain unconvinced by McLuhan's reasons for eschewing a linear arrangement of his ideas, I shall try for the sake of the uninitiated reader to reduce his argument to that very form to which he so very violently objects.

To begin with, McLuhan claims, quite justifiably I think, that human experience is both plural and voluminous, and that in the very act of being conscious of ourselves we are in receipt of a rich manifold of simultaneous sensation. In any one moment of conscious time we are aware of sight, sound, smell, taste, and touch all at once. Any attempt to communicate this variegated experience from one mind to another entails simplifications and distortion; but, according to McLuhan, some methods of communication are better than others, depending on the degree to which the medium employed reproduces the full sensory variety of the original experience. The capacity of any given medium to perform in this way depends upon the number of sensory channels that it calls into action when working properly. The larger the number of senses involved, the better the chance of transmitting a reliable copy of the sender's mental state.

McLuhan believes that the spoken word answers these requirements more faithfully than any other medium. He holds this belief for two distinct reasons, one of which is more immediately acceptable than the other. On one hand he reminds us that although speech is designed to be heard, it is usually uttered in situations that call the other senses into play as well. That is to say, in order to make our spoken meaning clear we automatically use facial expressions and manual gestures; and we even use blows, grips, and caresses to emphasize our meaning still further. For this reason, if for no other, the spoken word activates the entire human sensorium and thereby underwrites the accuracy with which the spoken message reproduces the mental state to which it supposedly corresponds.

McLuhan also claims that the channel of hearing itself is intrinsically richer, or, as he puts it, "hotter," than that of sight, say. The result is that even if there were no other sensory clues coincident with the use of speech, the listener would still be in receipt of a richer, hotter message than one coming at him through the eye alone.

For both these reasons McLuhan claims that spoken language exerts an irresistible power over the listener's imagination and that words have acquired the status of what the philosopher Hermann Usener has called "momentary deities." Primitive man, who relies almost entirely on oral exchanges, lives therefore in a condition of rich imaginative enchantment, his mentality galvanized throughout the length and breadth of its sensory repertoire. According to McLuhan, the invention of writing violated this then sacred manifold and forced men to attend to vision at the expense of all the other sensory channels. To use a metaphor that McLuhan himself does not actually employ, the message transmitted by manuscript is like a symphonic melody picked out on the violin, while the same idea expressed in spoken words projects the condition of the full orchestral score.

The impoverishment brought about by the development of writing was magnified out of all proportion when writing was tidied up and mechanized by the invention of print. The brilliant legibility of type made it possible for the eye to race along the "macadamized" surface of a text, taking in at a careless glance notions that might be more subtly modulated and qualified when issued as an improvised speech. McLuhan also stresses the linear regularity of the printed page and claims that our long-standing exposure to such display has trained us to accept ideas only insofar as they conform to certain strict logical patterns. Gutenberg Man therefore is, by McLuhan's account, explicit, logical, and literal; by allowing himself to become overdisciplined by the closely ranked regiments of text, he has closed his mind to wider possibilities of imaginative expression.

McLuhan also points out that the visual uniformity of print constitutes a primitive model of industrial technology, and he asserts that by immersing ourselves in information that has been processed in this way we have inadvertently conditioned ourselves to accept, without knowing that we have done so, the dehumanizing tyranny of mechanical life. The man who lives in and through print submits without complaint to timetables, lists of weights and measures, formal instruction, and to all the other rationalized fiats of modern life. Gutenberg Man is punctual, productive, and expedient; and since, moreover, he now receives so much of his knowledge without ever having to face the individual human source, his sense of spiritual community has dwindled even as his technical mastery has flourished. In other words, McLuhan assumes the stance of a sophisticated Luddite, distinguishing himself from his machine-breaking predecessors by the way in which he points out that the discovery of printing was the original sin from which all the subsequent woes of industrial civilization are derived.

This is not to say that McLuhan views all technical ingenuity with the same suspicion. In fact, he sees the more recent developments in electronic technology as offering a God-sent escape from the slavery exerted by wheels and levers. For in a somewhat confused way he has identified the circuits of the electrical engineer with those of the human nervous system itself, and invites us to acknowledge that through television and radio we have given ourselves the opportunity of communicating with one another through media that can reproduce the plural simultaneity of thought itself. Through these media images and sounds can be flashed upon the attentive mind with telepathic speed; and, since the various mechanisms can be linked in a vast network, electronic man has reconvened the tribal village on a global scale.

Hence McLuhan's cheerful optimism in the face of cultural developments that have depressed and alarmed most of his colleagues. It is fair to point out, however, that McLuhan has been able to achieve this state of complacent euphoria only by stressing the immediate mental effect of the various media at the expense of neglecting the messages that they actually carry. This dissociation is made quite explicit by his notorious motto in which he asserts that the medium *is* the message. In fact, as we shall see later, McLuhan's intellectual career traces a dramatic arc from the position of a conventional literary critic happy to discuss the content of written text to that of a systems analyst who prefers to neglect the significance of *what* is said in favor of a study of the mechanical structures through which it is transmitted.

This partly accounts for the enthusiasm with which McLuhan has been appropriated by the practitioners of the mass media. Not only has an impressive academic figure cleared their name of the humiliating stigma of vulgar and destructive triviality; he has actually promoted them to the helm of cultural progress. And it is not just the practitioners of these arts that have been relieved of their cultural guilt; the audience also has been exonerated from the crime of self-indulgence. Intelligent spectators who would once have felt furtive about looking at television can now sit glued to their sets confident in the belief that by doing so they are participating in a new community of human self-interest. Not only that. So long as the viewers retain their vigilance and attend to the character of the media themselves (regardless of what is being said on them) they are actually pursuing the study of epistemology. In other words, McLuhan has convened an open university of the air at which to attend is to graduate; and in a world that is perhaps unduly impressed by academic credentials such an opening seems like a generous offer for every member of the viewing public to think of himself as active.

But in spite of all the objections that can be raised against the motto with which McLuhan's name has become associated, there is no doubt that the ability to detach the medium from the message has allowed him to look with a fresh eye at almost every other technical innovation by means of which men have extended the scope of mind and body. And although, of course, it is a gross exaggeration to claim that the medium *is* the message, the medium *does* exert an effect over and above that which is carried in the message itself.

Take print as an example. We have become so familiar with the medium as such that we read the communiqués transmitted through it without pausing to consider the elaborate mental concessions that have to be made before we can accept and understand a message couched in serial phonetic symbols. If McLuhan's irritating motto does no more than render the text opaque for a moment, he has done a major service in making us conscious of the way in which so much of our knowledge is acquired.

The same technique of strategic exaggeration also pays dividends in other areas of technological history. Wheels, clothes, money, movies, and photos all embody psycho-

logical assumptions that are larger than the acknowledged purpose of the inventions themselves. McLuhan
may resort to some maddening tricks of paradox and
pun in order to make this point—money, for example,
being the poor man's credit card—but he has at least
forced a large audience to recognize the way in which
technical innovation creates psychological environments,
environments to which we subordinate ourselves without
clearly recognizing the price we pay in doing so.

It is often assumed that McLuhan's enterprise is
unique and that he has emerged fully fledged from an
egg that has no parents. In fact, his approach to cultural
history has well-established precedents, and in the discussion that follows I shall try to locate McLuhan's work
in the tradition to which it belongs. Moreover, it would
be a mistake to imagine that McLuhan arrived at his
well-known positions all of a sudden. Just as his notions
have an ancestry within the history of ideas, so do they
have a personal biography; and in the course of what follows I shall try to show the somewhat circuitous path he
has followed in order to arrive at such defensive assertions. For the purpose of discussion I have deliberately
adopted a hostile tone, partly, I must admit, because I
am in almost complete disagreement with the main body
of McLuhan's ideas, but partly too in order to lend a certain rhetorical vigor to the discussion. My medium is
part of my message.

The Underlying Values

i

For someone who has made such a spectacular success of dramatizing his public work, Marshall McLuhan remains unexpectedly quiet on the subject of his personal development. In interviews he tends to dismiss biographical questions and prefers to wrap his intellectual past in deliberate mystery. It would be easy, perhaps, to ignore this reticence as an irrelevant quirk if examination of his written work did not reveal that his autobiographical silence is closely related to his central thesis. For according to him the very idea of personal authorship is a dangerous artifact brought about by the invention of printing. When knowledge was communicated by word of mouth, or else by handwritten manuscript, the wisdom that accumulated in the public domain was wholesomely anonymous, and therefore much more comprehensive, than that which was later cut up and distributed between individual named authors who stood to gain substantial royalties by signing texts that could now be reproduced in profitable numbers.

However, it was not just the economic incentive offered by print that helped to split up the written truth into privately owned opinions; the physical medium itself, by virtue of some mysterious influence that it exerted on the human mind, restricted the mental vision to a fixed point of view. "It is upon this fixed point of view that the triumphs and destructions of the Gutenberg Era will be made." I continue to find this argument obscure and unconvincing, but McLuhan himself is sufficiently moved by it to try to offset the proprietary and therefore restrictive effects of print in his own work, committed though he is to publishing himself in the medium he so deeply suspects. By remaining enigmatic on the subject of his past he has tried to depersonalize his own enterprise and to represent its results, not as privately owned opinions, but as orphan data sent back to earth, as it were, from an unmanned space probe. The metaphor of the probe occurs with increasing frequency in those recent interviews where he attempts to justify his peculiar style, and it is apparent that he likes to see himself, not as an author, but as a publicly subsidized payload of sensitive instruments that records information irrespective of personal values. Take, for instance, these passages from McLuhan's interview with G. E. Stearn:

> I'm perfectly prepared to scrap any statement I ever made about any subject once I find it isn't getting me into the problem. I have no devotion to any of my probes as if they were sacred opinions. I have no proprietary interest in my ideas and no pride

of authorship as such. You have to push any idea to an extreme, you have to probe. . . .

Now values, insofar as they register a preference for a particular kind of effect or quality, are a highly contentious and debatable area in every field of discourse. Nobody in the twentieth century has ever come up with any meaningful definition or discussion of "value." . . . It is rather fatuous to insist upon values if you are not prepared to understand how they got there and by what they are now being undermined. The mere moralistic expression of approval or disapproval, preference or detestation, is currently being used in our world as a substitute for observation and a substitute for study. People hope that if they scream loudly enough about "values" then others will mistake them for serious, sensitive souls who have higher and nobler perceptions than ordinary people.[1]

As I will show later, McLuhan justifies the attitude expressed in these quotations by referring to the intellectual success achieved by modern artists who also repudiate, in one way or another, the tyranny of a single point of view. In cubism, for instance, the painter gains an all-round view of visual reality denied to those who insist upon depicting objects from a privileged viewpoint. Likewise the rich allusive plurality of symbolism or surrealism is only achieved by opening the mind to the largest number of simultaneous imaginative options. By analogy with the success of such aesthetic endeavors McLuhan tends to cast suspicions upon any form of investigation that allows "values" or anything else to limit the lines of inquiry.

[1] Gerald Emanuel Stearn, ed., *McLuhan Hot and Cool* (New York: Dial, 1967), p. 320.

Now although these are the terms in which McLuhan overtly seeks to vindicate his peculiar contempt for "values," I believe that it is possible to make out an additional motive of which he, as an author, is not immediately aware. For one can recognize in McLuhan's words to Stearn a pastiche of the idiom that is commonly attributed to experimental scientists. It is frequently thought that the impressive weight of scientific truth is gained at the expense of sacrificing commitment to personal opinion and that the good scientist is no more than a sensitive antenna tuned to pick up facts and figures as they occur. If one does conceive of science in this way, and many laymen do, it is quite natural to be suspicious of any attitude or interest that might limit the sensitivity of the antenna or probe.

In yielding to such suspicions, McLuhan has dangerously misconceived the role of so-called detached observation in science. For the "unprejudiced" accumulation of hard facts, in the manner suggested by Francis Bacon, plays very little part in the development of what we now recognize as science. Quite apart from the fact that heaps of data can never on their own add up to make a theory, it is unlikely that we would ever know where to begin looking unless a foregoing set of personal preferences gave us a criterion by which to choose the incidents that would be relevant to observe. As Sir Karl Popper observes,

> The belief that science proceeds from observation to theory is still so widely and so firmly held that my denial of it is often met with incredulity. I have even been suspected of being insincere—of denying what nobody in his senses can doubt.
> But in fact the belief that we can start with pure

observations alone, without anything in the nature
of a theory, is absurd. . . . Observation is always
selective. It needs a chosen object, a definite task,
an interest, a point of view, a problem. And its
description presupposes a descriptive language, with
property words; it presupposes interests, *points of
view*, and problems [my italics].[2]

Science starts out with heavily charged preconceptions
and only goes on to demonstrate its impartiality by its
willingness to abandon them in the face of acknowledged
refutation. While it is true that undue loyalty to certain
values may blind the investigator to observations that
would otherwise threaten his preconceptions, to make a
wholesale repudiation of such attitudes in the belief that
by so doing one will automatically guarantee the truth of
one's theories is to misunderstand the fundamental logic
of scientific inquiry.

The same criticism holds for McLuhan's willingness
to abandon his probes as soon as they fail to get him
further "into the problem." Scientists do not abandon
their probes or theories so easily as that. As T. S. Kuhn
has recently pointed out, the surrender of an awkward or
otherwise unproductive theory is usually preceded by a
long period of ad hoc intellectual modification in the effort to save the hypothesis. When surrender finally does
occur it is only in favor of a new theory that significantly
overtakes the explanatory achievements of the previous
one. "Once a first paradigm through which to view nature
has been found, there is no such thing as research in the
absence of any paradigm. To reject one paradigm without simultaneously substituting another is to reject sci-

[2] Karl Popper, *Conjectures and Refutations* (London: Routledge, 1963), p. 46.

ence itself. That act reflects not on the paradigm but on the man. Inevitably he will be seen by his colleagues as 'the carpenter who blames his tools.' "[3] In other words, the abrupt unilateral surrender of a notion—call it a "probe" or whatever—far from being a proof of scientific integrity, is often just a sign of carelessness, boredom, or caprice.

McLuhan's claim to impartiality highlights a peculiar strain in his thought; for although he advertises a superlative freedom from "values," most of his work is founded upon an ardent wish to see certain very distinct ethical principles prevail. Revolted as he clearly is by the godless rationalism of science, he is at the same time vastly overawed by its current intellectual prestige. And in order to make his own arguments against it more impressive, he has adopted what he supposes to be the intellectual stance of the scientist, hoping in this way to defeat his opponents at their own game. Unhappily, he has assumed the stance without really understanding the rules with which it is associated and, like his coreligionist Teilhard de Chardin, succeeds thereby in impressing only those whose horror of science is equaled or surpassed by their susceptibility to its special jargon.

To compare McLuhan with Teilhard de Chardin would be unjust, but it is often useful to classify the varieties of intellectual folly and to show that apparently unrelated examples of bad thinking actually belong to certain well-recognized categories. McLuhan and Teilhard do belong to the same category, one which Sir Peter Medawar damned in his famous essay "The Phenomenon of Chardin":

[3] T. S. Kuhn, *The Structure of Scientific Revolutions* (Chicago: University of Chicago Press, 1962), p. 79.

The Phenomenon of Man is anti-scientific in temper (scientists are shown up as shallow folk skating about on the surface of things), and, as if that were not recommendation enough, it was written by a scientist, a fact which seems to give it particular authority and weight. Laymen firmly believe that scientists are one species of person. They are not to know that the different branches of science require very different aptitudes and degrees of skill for their prosecution. Teilhard practised an intellectually un-exacting kind of science in which he achieved a moderate proficiency. He has no grasp of what makes a logical argument or of what makes for proof. He does not even preserve the common decencies of scientific writing, though his book is professedly a scientific treatise.

It is written in an all but totally unintelligible style, and this is construed as prima facie evidence of profundity. It is because Teilhard has such wonderful *deep* thoughts that he's so difficult to follow —really, it's beyond my poor brain but doesn't that just *show* how profound and important it must be?[4]

Bracketing McLuhan with Teilhard is useful for an-other reason. It helps to expose an undeclared interest in McLuhan's thought. Like de Chardin, McLuhan is a Catholic, and although he makes no specific reference to the fact, it adds a hidden bias to all his famous opinions and thus makes nonsense of his claim to have freed him-self from the tyranny of "values." As I hope to show later, the bulk of McLuhan's work is strongly animated by Catholic piety and the bid for detachment is partly a tac-tical stance designed to deceive "the enemy."

[4] Peter B. Medawar, *The Art of the Soluble* (London: Methuen, 1967), pp. 79–80.

Strangely enough, Catholicism itself offers its adherents an opportunity for assuming the very detachment McLuhan seeks, for one can recognize in the *social* situation of the Anglo-American Catholic a sense of alienation that strongly compensates for any "point of view," a situation that McLuhan summed up in an essay on Hopkins: "Long accustomed to a defensive position behind a minority culture, English and American Catholics have developed multiple mental squints. Involuntarily their sensibilities have been nourished and ordered by a century or more of an alien literary and artistic activity which, faute de mieux, they still approach askance."[5]

For someone who, like McLuhan, has a vested interest in disclaiming the bias associated with a "single point of view," any institution that can incidentally set up "multiple squints" immediately recommends itself for reasons that are distinct from, and even opposed to, the creeds of the institution itself.

The same paradox holds true for McLuhan's Canadian nationality. There are very strong "points of view" associated with the region of Canada in which McLuhan was raised—agrarian distributist ideas that form, along with his Catholicism, the main underlying motive in the work that has made him famous. At the same time, however, there is in the Canadian experience at large such a conflict of cultural and social identities that anyone interested in exploiting them could develop all the "mental squints" necessary to offset the dangers of a "single point of view."

Like his counterpart in the United States, the Canadian intellectual has an equivocal relationship with the mother culture of Europe. While he is relieved of what he sometimes considers to be the dead weight of its effete

[5] "The Analogical Mirrors," p. 21.

tradition, he is also envious of its complex, living heritage. His spirit may be broadened and invigorated by the wide-open spaces, but at the same time it is starved of the richer details upon which the mature critical imagination is nourished.

Such a deep split in cultural loyalty would, on its own, protect the Canadian from the tyranny of a "single point of view." But he suffers or enjoys an additional squint by virtue of his ambiguous attitude toward the United States. While he cannot fail to identify himself with the flourishing fortunes of North America as a whole, he is proud to distinguish a unique Canadian destiny whose rugged purity, as he sees it, reproves the luxurious materialism of the United States. Add to this the pains of French separatism and one can readily appreciate that in Canada McLuhan might well have found an ideal situation within which to develop the multiple viewpoints that he considers so favorable to critical impartiality.

I don't want to overstress the urge toward detachment. It is more important to identify the "values" that the carefully assumed detachment conceals, and this requires, in the first instance, an examination of early influences on his thought.

Marshall McLuhan was born and brought up in the western provinces of Canada. As a result he fell quite naturally under the influence of social ideas that have continued to shape both the imagination and the political initiative of the American Northwest since the early years of the nineteenth century. Loosely speaking, one can group these ideas under the single heading of agrarian socialism, bearing in mind that this political category covers a wide variety of beliefs, some of which are direct contradictions of others.

From the earliest days of westward migration into the great American prairies, the pioneers had been urged on-ward by the dream of a garden utopia within which any man who was willing to mix his labor with the soil could realize the invigorating ideals of sturdy yeoman inde-pendence:

> We are a people of cultivators . . . united by the silken bands of mild government, all respecting the laws, without dreading their power, because they are equitable. We are all animated with the spirit of an industry which is unfettered and unrestrained, because each person works for himself. If he travels through our rural district he views not the hostile castle, and the haughty mansion, contrasted with the clay-built hut and miserable cabin, where cattle and men help to keep each other warm, and dwell in meanness, smoke and indigence. A pleasing uni-formity of decent competence appears throughout our habitations. . . . Lawyer or merchant are the fairest titles our towns afford; that of a farmer is the only appellation of the rural inhabitants of our country.[6]

In spite of the painful practical experience that tended to undermine this joyful belief, the myth of simple yeo-man independence continued to animate the Western imagination; even today, when the social and demo-graphic circumstances under which it might have been realized have vanished altogether, the myth survives to give color to the rhetoric of the American radical Right.

Quite apart from the immediate difficulties associated with the terrain itself, the agrarian ideal came into seri-ous conflict with reality when, by the middle of the nine-

[6] J. Hector St. John de Crèvecœur, *Letters from an American Farmer* (1782) (London: Dent, 1962), pp. 40–41.

teenth century, Eastern capitalism began to extend its influence over the economics of the Middle Western wheat belts. Railroads that were controlled from New York determined the transport facilities for marketing the crop, and distant bankers manipulated the debts that the farmers incurred while purchasing new equipment. Far from being free, the nineteenth-century yeoman farmer was becoming helplessly dependent upon the behavior of a remote economic system over which he had no direct control.

In an effort to preserve the myth that had first prompted them to move west, the farmers began to organize programs of rural protest, by means of which they sought to restore their economic individuality. Independent or reform parties were founded in the attempt to control both the monopolies of the railroads and the franchises of the various middlemen. Later came the Greenback parties, whose main aim was to exempt the farmer from the whimsical credit restrictions of the Eastern banks. Neither these nor subsequent movements ever succeeded in producing a major change in the political structure of the American West, and in fact it was only in western Canada that agrarian radical politics achieved any serious legislative status, and not until the twentieth century. In Saskatchewan the Co-operative Commonwealth Federation did succeed in gaining majority power in the 1930s; and as Martin Lipset points out, it did so in the same geographical area that had earlier produced the Greenbackers, the Populists, and other agrarian upheavals.

This short sketch of Canadian political agrarianism is enough to indicate the sort of ferment within which the young McLuhan grew up. By the time he arrived in England as a postgraduate student in English studies at

Cambridge he was thoroughly imbued with distributist ideals that he continued to nurse, finally developing them in a subtly disguised form in such publications as *The Gutenberg Galaxy*, which seem on the surface to be no more than dispassionate accounts of the effects of new technologies upon the senses of man.

It is easy, therefore, to understand the sympathy which the young McLuhan felt for the severe agrarian partialities of the Cambridge critic F. R. Leavis.

> This strength of English [wrote Leavis] belongs to the very spirit of the language—the spirit that was formed when the English people who formed it were predominantly rural. . . . And how much richer the *life* was in the old, predominantly rural order than in the modern suburban world. . . . When one adds that speech in the old order was a popularly cultivated art, that people talked (so making Shakespeare possible) instead of reading or listening to the wireless, it becomes plain that the promise of regeneration by American slang, popular idiom, or the invention of *transition*-cosmopolitans is a flimsy consolation for our loss.[7]

A modern reader, unacquainted with McLuhan's prairie background, could be forgiven for failing to see the connection between this sort of rhetoric and the ideas expressed in works like *Understanding Media*. Quite apart from its well-advertised "detachment," McLuhan's later work does not immediately read as if it had been produced by anyone who favored the robust organic simplicities of village life. The text bristles with "scientific" terms, and the whole inquiry seems to be framed by a general interest in the behavior of the nerv-

[7] F. R. Leavis, *For Continuity* (London: Gordon Frazer Minority Press, 1933), p. 217.

ous system. If one were looking for *any* Cambridge antecedents to this later work, one would be tempted to scrutinize not the moral formulations of Leavis but the positivist work of I. A. Richards. It is therefore essential to make a brief digression in order to map out the intellectual character of Cambridge in the early 1930s.

The international reputation of Cambridge in the 1930s rested very largely on scientific achievements, the most spectacular of which were the nuclear investigations of Rutherford and his associates. While the atom was yielding up its secrets in the Cavendish Laboratory, biologists were beginning to secure vast theoretical dividends by subjecting the nervous system to the newly available techniques of electrophysiology. Shortly before World War I, for example, Keith Lucas had laid the foundations for describing the code in terms of which information was transmitted through the living nervous system. Although Lucas was killed in an air crash before he could complete his work, his student and colleague E. D. Adrian later achieved world fame for describing some of the simpler grammar and punctuation of this code. The neural medium was beginning to reveal its messages.

Meanwhile the school of experimental psychology under the leadership of men like C. S. Myers and W. H. R. Rivers was trying to quantify the subjective aspects of human experience—in spite of the fact that when the idea of a psychophysical laboratory was first suggested at the end of the previous century it had been opposed by the Cambridge Senate on the grounds that it would insult religion by putting the human soul on a pair of scales! This objection was soon dismissed, and I mention it in this context only because it echoes McLuhan's own equivocations on the subject and reminds us of the way in which his passion for neuropsychological mottoes goes hand in hand with a hatred for the way in which quantitative science has abused the integrity of the human spirit.

One of the most important incidents in the development of the Cambridge psychology school was the anthropological expedition that the zoologist Haddon led to the Torres Straits in 1898. Both Myers and Rivers were appointed to this excursion, and for the first time in history the primitive mind was laid open to the scrutiny of quantitative experimental science. Under the influence of this experience Rivers turned to the study of ethnology and psychiatry, and in the early 1920s completed some of the first English work on the manipulations of symbols and myths by the unconscious mind. Under his guidance, the psychologist F. C. Bartlett followed a similar path and, two years before McLuhan arrived in Cambridge, published a book called *Remembering* in which he demonstrated the way in which experiences are edited and reshaped by the memory.

It seems unlikely that McLuhan ever came into immediate contact with the work of these pioneers; and the mere fact that their joint enterprises were flourishing shortly before he arrived in Cambridge does not on its own prove that he was influenced by them. Nevertheless, there is a remarkable coincidence between the scope of their interests and the way in which McLuhan subsequently brought anthropology and neurology into his discussions. One might be tempted to dismiss this as mere coincidence were it not for the fact that I. A. Richards, a particularly eloquent member of the English school, had yielded to the direct influence of these scientific studies of the human mind not long before McLuhan's arrival in Cambridge.

Richards's work was in fact the culmination of a revolution that took place in English studies just after World War I. Before then the study of English had been no more than a small section within the Modern Language Tripos, but in 1917 it was recognized as a department on its own and by the middle 1920s critics such as M. D. Forbes had begun a successful bid to liberalize a province that had previously been divided between philological scholarship and vague laudatory criticism. Of the latter the English critic E. M. W. Tillyard wrote, in a memoir that provides a fascinating insight into the history of the Cambridge English school, "Although it contains better things than people are now likely to allow, the dominant trend was towards gossipy, and often highly metaphorical, description and unspecific praise; unspecific for, since imaginative writing was an affair of the emotions alone and the emotions do not lend themselves to analysis, you merely evade the issue if you enter into great detail."[8]

Tillyard confesses that by this time he had become impatient of such criticism, preferring with Forbes to stick closely to the texts and to find there, by a process of close analysis, the precise reasons for their effects. These ambitions achieved a special cutting edge when Forbes and Tillyard joined forces with I. A. Richards, who had lately emerged with honors from the school of Moral Science and Philosophy.

Cambridge philosophy was turning away from German idealism and, under the influence of Russell, Moore, and

[8] E. M. W. Tillyard, *The Muse Unchained* (London: Bowes & Bowes, 1958), p. 84.

Wittgenstein, was achieving international fame by investigating the logical structure of meaning itself. As Tillyard points out, Richards was responsible, more than anyone else, for developing in literature the philosophical empiricism of Moore; and in order to do this he never hesitated to include work that was current in both experimental psychology and anthropology.

By the time McLuhan arrived in Cambridge, Richards was already famous for promoting the idea that literature could be profitably regarded as a special example of the neural manipulation of artificial signs; and for suggesting moreover that practical criticism would be re-established on a firm footing of positivism if only we could analyze the way in which the nervous system processes and assimilates the information provided for it by the imaginative writer. The promises held out by this program now seem somewhat innocent and overoptimistic, but for all that Richards had undoubtedly made an impressive bid to restore the study of human communication to the larger province of epistemology.

In this respect at least McLuhan's work seems, on the surface, to be a natural outcome of what he had learned as a research student in Cambridge. McLuhan, however, now denies that Richards played any significant part in directing his subsequent interest toward the behavior of the nervous system. And although the coincidence of interests is rather remarkable, one should not be distracted by it from seeing that McLuhan exploits the data of psychology and anthropology in a very personal manner. For while Richards uses scientific information in order to compile a descriptive grammar of the literary response, McLuhan uses—and in many cases abuses— the same data in order to derive a prescription for a healthy and rounded spiritual life. For McLuhan, in the final reduction, takes a theological view of the human mentality, regarding it as the organ through which men achieve or fail to achieve their cognitive communion with God's creation. In other words, he has already decided what the proper function of human knowledge should be; and he judges its various conditions according to whether or not it matches up to this theologically determined ideal.

It would be a mistake, then, to overstress the affinity between McLuhan and Richards, for while McLuhan acknowledges the contribution that Richards's method has made to the understanding of literature, he insists that Leavis overtops it by virtue of the integral supremacy of his moral vision. As he wrote in 1944:

> In a word, then, the method of Leavis has superior relevance to that of Richards [and Empson] because he has more clearly envisaged not only the way in which a poem functions, but the function of poetry as well. A poem in itself functions dramatically, not strategically or persuasively. It is for contemplation, and functions for the spectator or reader as a means of extending and refining moral perception or dramatic awareness. Where Mr. Leavis sees the function of poetry as the education or nourishment of the affections, Richards [and Empson] tend to regard it pragmatically and rhetorically as a means of impinging on a particular situation. Since the material or vehicle of all art is necessarily social symbol and experience, Richards [and Empson] have done a great service by insisting on the discriminating perception of the complex implications of this matter. They have made art respectable and redoubtable once more for all intelligent men. So much so that it is tempting to take up permanent residence in their halfway house and to overlook the arduous stage of

the journey which remains to be accomplished before winning an overall view, which is plenary critical judgment.[9]

Moreover, Leavis's agrarian opinions coincide very closely with those of all other writers on whom McLuhan looked with favor for expressing disgust at the quality of life in the twentieth century. This nostalgic despair is generally associated with a tradition that Stephen Spender accurately characterized as follows:

> From Carlyle, Ruskin, Morris and Arnold, to T. E. Hulme, Ezra Pound, Yeats, Eliot, Lawrence and Leavis, there is the search for a nameable boojum or snark that can be held responsible for splitting wide apart the once fused being-created consciousness. . . . There runs through modern criticism the fantasy of a Second Fall of Man. The First Fall, it will be remembered, had the result of introducing Original Sin into the world of Man, exiled from the Garden of Eden, and knowing good and evil. The Second Fall seems to result from the introduction of scientific utilitarian values and modes of thinking into the world of personal choice between good and evil, with the result that values cease to be personal and become identified with the usefulness or destructiveness of social systems and material things.[10]

Throughout his life, both in essays and in his full-length books, McLuhan has continued to promote many of these authors, especially the ones who are associated with what is now recognized as the "modern" movement —Pound, Eliot, Yeats, and Joyce. However, when McLuhan first expressed public favor for this tradition he did

[9] "Poetic vs. Rhetorical Exegesis," p. 276.
[10] Stephen Spender, *The Struggle of the Modern* (London: Methuen, 1965), p. 26.

so by praising an author whose criticisms of modern life were much more boisterous and a great deal less sophisticated than those made by the tenants of Axel's Castle. In 1936 he wrote a short essay in which he loudly sponsored G. K. Chesterton for "being concerned to maintain our endangered institutions" and "for seeking to re-establish agriculture and small property as the only free basis for a free culture."

To McLuhan the world of G. K. Chesterton was

> rigid with thought and brilliant with colour . . . the very antithesis of the pale-pink lullaby-land of popular science. It is the difference between a cathedral window and blank infinity. That is why modern life, thoughtless and unpoised, has degenerated from a dance into a race, and history is regarded as a toboggan slide. But Mr. Chesterton has exposed the Christless cynicism of the supposedly iron laws of economics, and has shown that history is a road that must often be reconsidered and even retraced. For, if Progress implies a goal, it does not imply that all roads lead to it inevitably. And today, when the goal of Progress is no longer clear, the word is simply an excuse for procrastination. . . .
>
> The extraordinary extent and variety of his writings and discussions is proportioned to the desperate need for direction and unity in an age that has "smothered man in men." For external complexity has produced an insane simplification of thought, preying upon personal variety and spontaneous social expression.[11]

But is Chesterton's argument as "rigid with thought" as McLuhan claims it is? It is certainly colorful, and the famous paradoxes resound with all the clangor of

[11] "G. K. Chesterton: A Practical Mystic," pp. 457, 461.

newly minted thought. And yet beneath the vituperative surface of the prose there is nothing that could properly be called a political idea. Take for instance these passages:

> Certainly, it would be far better to go back to village communes, if they really are communes. Certainly, it would be better to do without soap rather than to do without society. Certainly, we would sacrifice all our wires, wheels, systems, specialities, physical science and frenzied finance for one half-hour of happiness such as has often come to us with comrades in a common tavern. I do not say the sacrifice will be necessary; I only say it will be easy. . . .
>
> Perhaps the truth can be put most pointedly thus: that democracy has one real enemy, and that is civilisation. Those utilitarian miracles which science has made are anti-democratic, not so much in their perversion, or even in their practical result, as in their primary shape and purpose. The Frame-Breaking Rioters were right; not perhaps in thinking that machines would make fewer men workmen; but certainly in thinking that machines would make fewer men masters. More wheels do mean fewer handles; fewer handles do mean fewer hands. The machinery of science must be individualistic and isolated. A mob can shout round a palace; but a mob cannot shout down a telephone. The specialist appears, and democracy is half spoilt at a stroke.[12]

Although Chesterton confidently titled the book from which these passages are taken *What's Wrong with the World*, it is hard to summarize the diagnosis that has supposedly been given. According to McLuhan, however, Chesterton gave his own summary:

[12] G. K. Chesterton, *What's Wrong with the World* (London: Cassell, 1910), pp. 109, 99–100.

We have hands that fashion and heads that know,
But our hearts we lost—how long ago!

In other words, Chesterton claims that by submitting ourselves to the tyranny of the machine and by putting our trust in rationalism we have crowned the head, vanquished the heart, and thereby lost the habit of perfection. In some ways this is an attractive myth—it is in fact a common theme in early twentieth-century writing—and it is easy to see why the young Canadian distributist was drawn to it. It is harder, however, to keep patience with anyone who could continue to sponsor such a primitive fantasy. Yet the head-heart split still features in McLuhan's modern work, and in *The Gutenberg Galaxy* it takes pride of place among the explanations of our modern predicament.

The difficulty is that the distinction between head and heart, as Chesterton and McLuhan recognize it, is so vague and so metaphorical that it has no legitimate place in what can properly be called an explanation. For there is not, and cannot be, a reliable criterion by which to distinguish effects that arise from the "head" as opposed to those that are prompted by the "heart." Even to imagine that there might be is to fall into the same logical error that doomed the phrenologists. For the distinction itself arises from a corrupt psychological theory according to which the human personality is partitioned into discrete faculties, organs, or ministries, each separately responsible for a certain class of behavior or awareness. Such serious inconsistencies appear when one traces this theory back to its logical origin that it would be unwise to base a social explanation upon it. Unfortunately, both Chesterton and McLuhan seem unaware of the logical quagmire upon which their proposal is raised.

Even if the distinction between head and heart *had* more respectable foundations, it would be hard to characterize satisfactorily any given historical period in terms of it. Chesterton and McLuhan would presumably maintain that the head was gracefully subordinated to the heart in the early part of the Middle Ages—in which case it seems odd that so many humane initiatives should have borne fruit in the period when the head was gaining its deadly precedence over the heart, i.e. in the last hundred years. Both Chesterton and McLuhan would save their theory by simply refusing to admit that these initiatives were examples of the heart in action. "Current sociology and social engineering," McLuhan wrote in 1946, "so far from being a source of hope or renewal of impulse must themselves be studied as morbid symptoms. The most hopeful developments in social thought have . . . been in the direction of exploring modes of thought and feeling rather than in the quarter where mechanical efforts to tinker the good society into existence have prevailed."[13]

In other words, our only hope is to cultivate the faculty of intuition, by whose benevolent workings we shall, in Chesterton's words, remember "what we really are." Rationality is just a snare and a delusion. "All that we call common sense and rationality and practicality and positivism only means that for certain dead levels of our life we forget that we have forgotten. All that we call spirit, art and ecstasy only means that for one awful instant we remember that we forget."[14]

It is important to realize here that, to a large extent,

[13] "Footprints in the Sands of Crime," p. 619.
[14] G. K. Chesterton, *Orthodoxy* (London: John Lane, Bodley Head, 1909), p. 95.

both McLuhan's and Chesterton's hostility to social engineering is prompted by Catholic piety. For if you hold that human nature is blemished by Original Sin, it is, of course, idle to suppose that pain and evil will ever be dissipated by simply changing the secular institutions of society in accordance with rational principles. Since the discontents of civilization arise from a metaphysical flaw in human nature, men can only hope to obtain relief from their misery and confusion by submitting themselves to the mystery of God's redeeming intervention, and by cultivating those modes of intuition through which they can become aware of such a redemptive opportunity.

Even if they are not conceived to be in direct antagonism to one another, piety and rational philanthropy coexist within the religious imagination in a state of strong reciprocal tension, and the Catholic often believes that the condensed symbolic mystery of the Incarnation will be dispersed if one tries to translate its ineffable benevolence into any overt acts of institutionalized good will. McLuhan's rubric expresses this anxiety in a rather brusque and dismissive manner; the same idea is put more delicately perhaps by a Catholic anthropologist who has recently confessed to unease at the way in which pious ritual has been weakened by attempts to alleviate human misery through concrete acts of social welfare, unmediated by sacred ritual.

> There is no person whose life does not need to unfold in a coherent symbolic system. The less organised the way of life, the less articulated the symbolic system may be. But social responsibility is no substitute for symbolic forms and indeed depends upon them. When ritualism is openly despised the philanthropic

impulse is in danger of defeating itself. For it is an illusion to suppose that there can be organisation without symbolic expression.[15]

As I hope to show in a later section, McLuhan has identified the progressive inability of modern man to express his piety through natural symbols with the growth of literal thought as it was encouraged by printing; and as the argument develops I hope to show how his investigations of the new media are prompted in a very large measure by his eagerness to find a new form of iconic symbolism through which the redemptive mysteries of God can be experienced.

[15] Mary Douglas, *Natural Symbols* (London: Barrie & Rockliff, 1970), p. 50.

North and South

● ●

11

It is hard to say how the influence of Chesterton on McLuhan would have prospered if McLuhan had returned to Canada on leaving Cambridge in 1936. But instead of going straight home he spent the next decade teaching English at the Catholic university in St. Louis; and although Missouri is, strictly speaking, a Midwestern state, it borders on the South, so that by living and working there McLuhan came into very close contact with a form of agrarianism that reinforced what he had admired in Chesterton but marked at the same time a significant departure from what he had known in western Canada.

At the level of sentimental rhetoric there is, of course, a striking similarity between the agrarianism of the South and that of the American Northwest. Both rejoice in the spiritual dignity of labor:

Those who labour in the earth [wrote Thomas Jefferson] are the chosen people of God, if ever He had a chosen people, whose breasts He has made his peculiar deposit for substantial and genuine virtue. It is the focus in which He keeps alive that sacred fire, which otherwise might escape from the face of the earth. Corruption of morals in the mass of cultivators is a phenomenon of which no age nor nation has furnished an example. . . . While we have land to labour then, let us never wish to see our citizens occupied at a workbench, or twirling a distaff. . . . The mobs of great cities add just so much to the support of pure government as sores do to the strength of the human body.[1]

Many Southern intellectuals came to suspect this optimistic formula, and did so, moreover, many years before their prairie counterparts—George Fitzhugh of Virginia, for example—saw quite clearly that the Georgic pleasures of the soil could only be enjoyed by those who had been relieved of its necessary toil by their black slaves. The upshot was that although the South and the prairies entered the nineteenth century in loose political alliance against the industrial Northeast, the two regions fell out in the 1850s when the Midwestern states offended their Southern colleagues by repudiating the use of slavery. Henceforth Southern agrarianism became distinctively associated not so much with the yeoman ideal as with that of a graceful landed aristocracy. By the time the Civil War broke out Southerners had consolidated a romantic image of their own peculiar virtues, through the contemplation of which they unconsciously sought to vindicate the "peculiar institution" of slavery.

[1] Thomas Jefferson, *Notes on the State of Virginia* (Chapel Hill, N.C.: University of North Carolina Press, 1955), pp. 157–58.

Modern historians have questioned the reality of this comforting legend. For the Old South was never, in fact, the graceful patrician paradise imagined by its more enthusiastic publicists. Most of its people were drawn from lower- and middle-class stock, many of them Irish and Scots. There were small enclaves of English gentry, but many of these were relatively uncouth country squires, not to be confused with the Cavalier aristocracy of popular myth. When Frederick Olmstead visited the antebellum South he was appalled by the grasping parvenu vulgarity of its inhabitants.

Nevertheless it would be foolish to disregard the myth simply because it did not square with social reality. Myths can often change behavior in the direction of the norms they embody; and even if the image of corporate chivalry was scarcely more than a fantasy, it probably achieved a measure of reality by regularizing the conduct of those who felt it to be true.

Whatever foundation in reality the myth may once have had, it was destroyed once and for all by the Civil War and by the social upheavals of the Reconstruction that followed. Crude economic reality forced the Southerners to abandon the attempt to create a society based upon elementary agriculture, with the result that the control of society shifted from the agricultural aristocracy to men of industry and commerce. But in spite of economic and social upheaval, or, to be more accurate, because of it, the myth of ancient *noblesse oblige* continued to survive in the imagination of the defeated Southerners. Publicists such as Henry W. Grady enthusiastically announced the birth of a New South that was to be based upon a modern industry competitive with that of the Yankee North; and hopeful nostalgists consoled themselves for this unwelcome change with the belief that

the chivalrous virtues of the Old South would revive concurrently with the new lease of life about to be conferred upon their defeated nation.

Not that Southern intellectuals of the early 1920s
cared much either way. Most of them realized that the
culture of the Old South was largely fictional. As for the
New South, they understood, no doubt, that the hap-
hazard introduction of industry was unlikely to create a
new culture where so little had existed before. So when
Allen Tate, John Crowe Ransom, Donald Davidson, and
others began to assemble what later became famous as
the Fugitive Group of Southern writers, their association was founded on nothing more militant than a joint
interest in the future of modern poetry. If anything, they
sought to dissociate themselves from the Southern literary tradition, insofar as it existed, and looked to Europe
for intellectual and aesthetic inspiration.

Most of these writers underestimated the strength of
their unconscious regional attachments, however, and
when the Scopes trial of 1925 brought down the contempt
and ridicule of Yankee journalists such as H. L. Mencken
and Westbrook Pegler, they discovered in themselves a
Southern loyalty that might otherwise have remained
dormant and finally vanished altogether. Moreover, they
were so outraged by the coarseness of Mencken's attacks
upon the South that they felt moved to collaborate in a
joint vindication of their homeland; and this impulse was
reinforced by the fact that many of them had already begun to nurse a fear and suspicion of Eastern industrialism.

In the three years that followed the trial, discussion
of the form that the vindication of the South should
take proved somewhat aimless. Tate and his colleagues
recognized that the *literary* tradition of the Old South

was too weak a structure upon which to base a defense of their region. Both Tate and Ransom turned instead to an advocacy of the regional life itself, and sought to point out the superiority of an existence that owed most of its richness and moral versatility to landed property and fixed social classes. In 1928 Tate published his famous biography *Stonewall Jackson, the Good Soldier*, in which he maintained that the sense of concrete moral obligation that arose quite naturally from direct ownership of land, and even of slaves, was superior to the abstract notion of right that plagued the politics of the rationalistic North.

Ransom, meanwhile, had completed and published an essay in which he suggested that the best chance for realizing plenary aesthetic fulfillment lay in the relaxed rural life of the Old South, and in 1929 Donald Davidson made an explicit appeal for contributions toward a corporate manifesto on behalf of the rural South. He asked that his friends should prepare a book "addressed to mature Southerners of the late nineteen twenties, in the so-called New South—Southerners who, we trusted, were not so far gone in modern education as to require for the act of comprehension, colored charts, statistical tables, graphs and journalistic monosyllables."

Books as well as articles promptly followed Davidson's call to action; and it is startling to recognize how closely this program of conservative defiance coincides with G. K. Chesterton's pious agrarianism—above all for the way in which the spiritual destitution of modern life is totally identified with the grammar of science, logic, and social statistics.

By recommending the South on account of superior piety and intuition, Davidson and the authors who were encouraged by him inadvertently shifted the emphasis of the debate. Although what followed may have seemed like an American conflict over competing local values, it actually rehearsed a much larger clash of temperaments, one that William James had identified in 1907:

> I think you will practically recognize the two types of mental make-up that I mean if I head the columns by the titles "tender-minded" and "tough-minded" respectively.

THE TENDER-MINDED	THE TOUGH-MINDED
Rationalistic	Empiricist
(going by "principles")	(going by "facts")
Intellectualistic	Sensationalistic
Idealistic	Materialistic
Optimistic	Pessimistic
Religious	Irreligious
Free-willist	Fatalistic
Monistic	Pluralistic
Dogmatical	Sceptical [2]

In the books and articles inspired by Davidson's call to action, most of the positions announced in the left-hand column of James's check list received polemic development. In 1929, for example, Ransom argued in *God Without Thunder* that religion, even fundamentalist religion, offered the only effective defense against progress, socialism, and the evils of the American economic system. By the same year, "Twelve Southern Writers" had assembled their defiant opinions in the now legendary anthology *I'll Take My Stand*.

Through the clamor of the joint diversity of these twelve writers came the single voice of "sensibility" and "intuition" defending itself against the tough-minded

[2] William James, *Pragmatism* (New York: Longmans, Green, 1907), pp. 11–12.

abstractions of scientific determinism. Two allied passages from Allen Tate's "Religion and the Old South" make the point:

> Religion, when it directs its attention to the horse cropping the blue-grass on the lawn, is concerned with the whole horse, and not with that part of him which he has in common with other horses, or that more general part which he shares with other quadrupeds or with the more general vertebrates; and not with the abstract horse in his capacity of horse-power in general, power that he shares with other machines of making objects move. Religion admits the existence of this horse, but says that he is only half of the horse. Religion offers to place before us the whole horse as he is in himself. . . .
>
> This modern mind sees only half of the horse— that half which may become a dynamo, or an automobile, or any other horse-powered machine. If this mind had much respect for the full-bodied, grass-eating horse, it would never have invented the engine which represents only half of him. The religious mind, on the other hand, has this respect; it wants the whole horse; and it will be satisfied with nothing less.[3]

See how closely this passage corresponds with one in Chesterton, where he praises the mystic for resisting the seductions of rational generalization:

> There is one element always to be remarked in the true mystic, however disputed his symbolism, and that is [his symbol's] brightness of colour and clearness of shape. I mean that we may be doubtful about the

[3] Allen Tate, "Religion and the Old South," *Reactionary Essays on Poetry and Ideas* (New York: Scribner's, 1936), pp. 168–69.

significance of a triangle or the precise lesson conveyed by a crimson cow. But in the work of a real mystic the triangle is a hard mathematical triangle not to be mistaken for a cone or a polygon. The cow is in colour a rich incurable crimson, and in shape unquestionably a cow, not to be mistaken for any of its evolutionary relatives, such as the buffalo or the bison. This can be seen very clearly, for instance, in the Christian art of illumination as practised at its best in the thirteenth and fourteenth centuries. The Christian decorators, being true mystics, were chiefly concerned to maintain the reality of objects. By plain outline and positive colour those pious artists strove chiefly to assert that a cat was truly in the eyes of God a cat and that a dog was pre-eminently doggish.[4]

It is significant in this context that Tate, Chesterton, and McLuhan share a deep religious affinity with mediaeval Christianity. In the illuminated manuscripts of the Middle Ages, McLuhan sees the last strongholds of primitive piety as it struggled with the profane rationalism encouraged by the invention of written characters; and when, ten years after the publication of *I'll Take My Stand*, he in turn came to defend the Southern style, he deliberately paraphrased Tate's appeal for the "whole horse." "The chivalric South, it has been said, wanted the whole horse, whereas the North wanted only to abstract the horsepower from the horse."[5]

Although like most sophisticated advocates of the Old South McLuhan had abandoned the historically unsupportable fiction of Dixie noblesse, he substituted for it

[4] G. K. Chesterton, *William Blake* (London: Duckworth, 1920), pp. 132 ff.
[5] "The Southern Quality," p. 375.

one that was equally wishful, suggesting that the South offered a splendid example of a society that shared its peculiar wisdom equally among all its members: "There is not the split between educated and 'uneducated' which occurs in an atomized industrial community . . . there is not the familiar head-heart split of the North, which became glaring in Europe and England in the Eighteenth Century."[6]

One cannot help wondering whether or not the Negro is supposed to be included in this exalted peerage. Perhaps not. Perhaps it is only by contrast with the supposed inferiority that prompts the Negro's unmentioned exclusion that the otherwise gross differences between educated and uneducated Southerners could be so promiscuously ignored. From Capetown to Montgomery the theory of unredeemable black inferiority has always been an unmentioned conceptual prerequisite for upholding the fiction of white equality.

I do not mean to suggest that McLuhan is a racist, or even that he exploits a racial theory in order to promote the impudent myth of Southern egalitarianism. I prefer to think that his error is created by a more general ignorance of social reality, and this diagnosis would account for many of the other mistakes in his social speculation. Although, for example, McLuhan in no way opposes the program of civil rights, he betrays an almost breathtaking naïveté when he comments on its achievements. "Many people have observed how the real integrator or leveler of White and Negro was the private car and the truck, not the expression of moral points of view." As Neil Compton exclaims, "Southern negroes will be astonished to learn that General Motors really de-

[6] *Ibid.*, p. 347.

serves the credit usually given to lunchroom sit-ins and voter-registration drives, and flabbergasted to note the tense in which McLuhan couches his remark."[7]

McLuhan is, then, so heavily prejudiced in favor of the agrarian ideal that he is perfectly willing to advertise the South as an example of it, even if he has to ride roughshod over contradictory facts. He is also an exponent of a bankrupt form of cultural history, the success of whose peculiar endeavor relies to a great extent on the

[7] Raymond Rosenthal, ed., *McLuhan Pro and Con* (New York: Funk & Wagnalls, 1968), p. 122.

To clinch the diagnosis of political ignorance in general I need only refer to an example taken from another area altogether.

McLuhan has always maintained that the cultural differences in "sensory emphasis" are one of the most important determinants of political behavior. In order to support this contention he sets up an unintentionally comic contrast between the espionage techniques employed respectively by the Russians and Americans. In *The Gutenberg Galaxy* he suggests that the Soviet preoccupation with "bugging" arises from the fact that Russia has always been an "ear" culture. The United States' preference for high-flying spotter planes betrays a characteristic American emphasis on the eye. In his enthusiasm for a theory that sets the eye against the ear, McLuhan has simply ignored the geopolitical facts. For example, it is a great deal easier to launch aerial missions around the frontiers of Russia when airstrips can be stationed on friendly territories nearby. The aerial surveillance of the island continent of America is a much riskier proposition altogether, entailing a dramatic violation of air space from which there is no immediate escape. Anyway, since *The Gutenberg Galaxy* was published, the growth of satellite technology has abolished this strategic inequality, and for all their supposed prejudice against the eye, the Russians have not been slow to pocket their ears in favor of the snapshots they can now obtain from orbiting spacecraft. And as for bugging, it was, after all, the CIA and not the NKVD who perfected the microphone concealed in the olive of an executive Gibson.

use of large-scale, tendentious generalizations. Even if McLuhan had *not* been an agrarian, he would have written the sort of history that ignored or else obliterated the otherwise incorrigible facts of economic and political reality. For McLuhan conceives human development on such a grand scale that its component social details are often foreshortened to the point where they become indistinguishable. The unique elements that comprise the living character of communities are either ignored altogether or, where they seem to fit, subordinated to such enormous generalizations that they cease to be usefully recognizable. History becomes a struggle between successive dynasties of synthetic Leviathans.

Writing history in this way encourages a Procrustean tendency whereby societies and the traditions that nourish them are identified only insofar as they conform to clear-cut and preferably sharply opposed ideological prototypes. Inconvenient exceptions that threaten to blur these neat distinctions are ignored altogether or translated into a form that corroborates the picture given. As a result, social reality loses its shape by being stretched between artificially paired alternatives.

Although this Procrustean tendency becomes dramatically marked only in his recent writings, which embody such tendentious distinctions as hot versus cool, eye versus ear, head against heart, McLuhan betrayed an early affinity for large-scale dualism in an essay of 1946 called "An Ancient Quarrel in Modern America." In this article and in the one on "The Southern Quality," McLuhan claimed to have identified an ancient intellectual schism that had survived through antiquity and the Renaissance to animate the modern conflict between the head and the heart.

This ideological split took its origin from the well-recognized quarrel between Socrates and the Sophists. Philosophers such as Protagoras had always maintained that the human senses were so fickle and unreliable that they could never penetrate the mystery of the physical universe. Absolute truth would always remain a dream, and the pursuit of science was therefore a waste of time. Nevertheless, while the Sophists were agreed that all human opinion was relative, they recognized that it was desirable, for the sake of civic harmony at least, that certain opinions should *prevail*. Instead of pursuing specialized knowledge, the Sophist advised the cultivation of prudential wisdom, and by encouraging the arts of persuasion and eloquence he tried to ensure popular obedience to the standards dictated by such wisdom. The Sophist emphasis fell therefore upon eloquence rather than curiosity; upon oratory as opposed to inquiry.

To Socrates and his followers this attitude represented a contemptible abdication of intellectual responsibility, and the Sophist was condemned as a glib, shallow publicist. In spite of such formidable opposition, the Sophist tradition survived to inspire the eloquent humanism of the Roman statesman Cicero. For this prudent patrician there seemed to be no contradiction between eloquence and wisdom. Man, after all, was distinguished from the beasts by his capacity to use language—by cultivating eloquence he could scarcely avoid becoming wiser.

For McLuhan, "the Ciceronian ideal reaches its flower in the scholar-statesman of encyclopaedic knowledge, profound practical experience and voluble social and public eloquence."[8] So successful was Cicero in promoting reconciliation among the separate roles of statesman, orator, and philosopher that he naturally became the

[8] "The Southern Quality," p. 371.

heroic ideal upon which the humanists of the Middle Ages and Renaissance modeled their own behavior.

> No more impressive evidence [wrote McLuhan] of the continuity of the "Ciceronian" tradition could be given here than that of L. K. Born in his preface of Erasmus' *Education of a Christian Prince*. Discussing the numerous manuals of this class, he says: That there is a continuous line of succession at least from the time of Isocrates with his *Ad Nicoclem* to the twentieth century is beyond question. The *Gargantua* of Rabelais is likewise a treatise on humanistic education for the prince just as much as More's *Utopia*, Castiglione's *Courtier*, Ascham's *Scholemaster*, and Spenser's *Faerie Queene*.[9]

In the eyes of such humanists there were no rewards for narrow technical specialism. How could there be? The mystery of nature was locked up forever, so what was the point of cultivating specialized skills that were doomed to failure from the start? By contrast with the delusion of absolute Truth, Prudence and Grace and Civility were the only practical ideals that a man could hope to achieve, and specialism of any sort would seriously jeopardize his chances of success.

This cult of humane integrity was first seriously threatened, according to McLuhan, when the Parisian scholar Peter Abelard revived the dialectical method in the twelfth century. Transmitted through the work of Ockham and the seventeenth-century Huguenot scholar Peter Ramus, Abelard's preoccupation with logical method reinfected Europe with the Socratic ambition to penetrate the scientific secrets of nature. The intellect achieved a dangerous precedence over the emotions, and men forgot their humanity in the drive to achieve tech-

[9] "An Ancient Quarrel in Modern America," pp. 149–50.

nical mastery over the universe around them. In gaining knowledge, man had forfeited wisdom. Only in the Southern states of America, where the humanistic ideal was "perfectly adapted to agrarian estate life," did the Sophist tradition survive with any genuine vigor. Elsewhere the head triumphed over the heart. In Calvinist New England, which had unfortunately inherited the specialized logic of Ramus, Harvard became a "miniature Sorbonne"; and henceforth the Yankees were condemned to fulfill the dreadful destiny of scientific industrialism. Suffering now from "an elephantiasis of the Will" and a corresponding atrophy of heartfelt civic prudence, the alienated Northerner was detached from the community around him, and hell-bent on profit and material fulfillment:

The tool of Ramistic scriptural exegesis proved very destructive of Scripture, naturally; for it was rationalistic and nominalistic. That is, it *made* all problems logical problems and at the same time destroyed *ontology* and any possibility of metaphysics, a fact which accounts for the notorious anemia, the paralyzing scepticism of New England speculation. Already in the Seventeenth Century Harvard had designated *technologia* as the true successor of metaphysics—an absurdity, with all the practical consequences, which is piously perpetuated at this hour by Dewey and his disciples. For this mind there is nothing which cannot be settled *by method*. It is the mind which weaves the intricacies of efficient production, "scientific" scholarship, and business administration. It doesn't permit itself an inkling of what constitutes a social or political problem (in the Burke or Yeats sense) simply because there is no *method* for tackling such problems. That is also why the very considerable creative political thought of America has come only from the South—from Jefferson to Wilson.[10]

Ramus plays an important part in McLuhan's historical speculations, and McLuhan finds in his writings a special relevance to his own typographic theory; it is important to understand why. Briefly then: Ramus opposed the logical method of Aristotle on the grounds that it was too cumbersome and almost impossible to memorize. He suggested that logical argument should be paid out in simple dichotomies, thus relieving the memory of the almost impossible task of fixing Aristotle's long lists of pedantically differentiated categories. It is difficult for a modern reader to imagine the advantages offered by such reforms. Even the improved dichotomies seem unnecessarily obscure, and it is hard to see how they could have assisted any important argument. However, the protagonists of the method were fanatically loyal to it, and the Calvinist academies of North America adopted it with great enthusiasm.

The problem of training and developing the human memory had been a major issue throughout antiquity and the Middle Ages, with authorities vying to produce the ideal mnemonic system. When Ramus projected his simplified scheme he was simply adding *his* contribution to a well-established tradition of mnemotechnics.

Most people are familiar with the fact that the memory is considerably assisted when the items to be recalled are arranged in the mind's eye in significant order, especially when that order is reinforced by vivid visual imagery.

[10] "The Southern Quality," p. 371.

I have been told of a professor [wrote Frances Yates] who used to amuse his students at parties by asking each of them to name an object; one of them noted down all the objects in the order in which they had been named. Later in the evening the professor would cause general amazement by repeating the list of objects in the right order. He performed his little memory feat by placing the objects, as they were named, on the window sill, on the desk, on the waste-paper basket, and so on. Then he revisited those places in turn and demanded from them their deposits. He had never heard of the classical mnemonic but had discovered his technique quite independently. Had he extended his efforts by attaching notions to the objects remembered on the places he might have caused still greater amazement by delivering his lectures from memory, as the classical orator delivered his speeches.[11]

This familiar technique was formally sponsored in two important treatises that came down to the Middle Ages from classical antiquity, the anonymous *Ad C Herennium Libri IV* and Cicero's *De Oratore*.

Consequently one must employ a large number of places which must be well lighted, clearly set out in order, at moderate intervals apart; and images which are active, sharply defined, unusual, and which have the power of speedily encountering and penetrating the psyche. . . . The ability to use these [images] will be supplied by practice which engenders habit, and [by images] of similar words changed and unchanged in case or drawn [from denoting] the part to denoting the genus, and by using the image of one word to remind of a whole sentence, as a consummate

[11] Frances Yates, *The Art of Memory* (London: Routledge, 1966), pp. 3–4.

painter distinguishing the position of objects by modifying their shapes.[12]

Methods such as these were earnestly recommended by scholars throughout the Middle Ages and Renaissance, since Memory was one of the crucial components of the cardinal virtue of Prudence. Ramus was offended by the concrete imagery suggested by Cicero and felt that it was unnecessary to stimulate the faculty of memory with such crude devices. He preferred to develop memory by encouraging the efficiency of rational thought itself. Logical consistency was its own guarantee of memorability. In this respect he was probably influenced by Quintilian, who had earlier criticized the visual method of Cicero, comparing it unfavorably with the advantages of straightforward unillustrated logical thinking.

According to McLuhan, however, it was not just the logical consistency of the arguments that helped them to remain in the memory, but the way in which they were laid out on the page. For although specific imagery had been banished from the method, the physical arrangement on the paper constituted a visual mnemonic in its own right, especially since it was displayed with the peculiar clarity possessed by print.

There are some disturbing inconsistencies in this proposal. Some impressive authorities disagree with the suggestion that Ramus's display technique depended upon the invention of printing, and that spatial visualization for memorization was a new development introduced by the printed book. And if, as McLuhan suggests, the visual sense was subordinate to the acoustic one before the invention of typography, the eloquent orator Cicero

[12] Cicero, *De Oratore*, trans. E. W. Sutton and H. Rackham (Cambridge, Mass.: Harvard University Press, 1942), II, lxxxvii, 357.

would surely have been the last person to sponsor the use of strong visual images as an *aide-mémoire*. And yet, in spite of the fact that Cicero lived long before the invention of type, he took extraordinary pains to acknowledge the primacy of sight among all the other senses.

The course of human development is so complex and so confusing that it is often tempting to accept schemes that appear to put the events of the last two thousand years into orderly and even elegant perspective. History, however, is incorrigibly resistant to such large-scale simplifications, and although it may be possible to identify *analogies* between the thoughts of one generation and the next, and even useful to draw tentative abstractions about the continuity of certain well-recognized traditions, it is dangerous to try to push the process farther than the real facts will allow. Conceptual simplicity is not necessarily a guarantee of truth, especially where human affairs are concerned.

How easy it would be to write history on the assumption that human development followed the course of a few relatively catastrophic divisions! After the crucial mutations that were responsible had been identified, the entire story of human progress could be redrawn on the plan of a family tree, and societies could then be confidently characterized according to whether or not they had inherited the fatal psychic genes. The difficulty is that the genetic model does not apply to social history, for the simple reason that the forces that determine social inheritance do not and cannot correspond to the simple fixed particles that are responsible for biological heredity. Such a model may provide an attractive metaphor, but in any attempt to reconstruct history on the assumption that it is anything more than a metaphor social details are brutally melted down until they can be poured into the convenient mold provided.

I am not competent to press hard upon all the errors that arise from McLuhan's technique—the dazzling scope of his reference makes it difficult for any one person to do so—but one or two critical objections at least make the larger point.

1. It is perverse to suggest that the humanistic tradition—even if one could realistically identify it as a continuous line—"benevolently" discouraged the growth of science. Most historians now agree, I think, that when experimental science began its substantial development in the seventeenth century, it actually *flourished* under the aegis of the humanism that first allowed men to look at nature without shuddering in metaphysical dread.

By systematically cultivating their status as human beings, men acquired such confidence in their own prudent nobility that they were no longer overawed by the competing majesty of nature. Far from *eclipsing* scientific curiosity, the image of civic order celebrated under the humanist regime provided a powerful metaphor through which men could confront nature as an orderly and explicable entity. If human affairs yielded so gracefully to decency and decorum, why shouldn't nature conform to the same benevolent plan? It is not an accident that the regularities of the cosmos should have been christened with the title of "Law."

I am not suggesting that all humanists incline toward science—far from. But it is absurd to imply that humanism itself constitutes the polar opposite of the temperament that *did* eventually concern itself with technical knowledge.

2. Although McLuhan sets up the humanistic cour-

tier as the ideal opponent of scientific specialism, this opinion hardly squares with the substantial patronage given to scientific academies by the princes of Renaissance Europe. Moreover, many of the exponents of seventeenth-century science were gentlemen of the very type McLuhan would have identified as antagonists of such an enterprise. William Harvey, for example, the paragon of experimental biology, was reared from the yeoman-agrarian stock that McLuhan so confidently appropriates to the tradition of antiscientific humanism. He spent the greater part of his life as a model courtier in the service of an Anglican monarch. And it was the Catholic Charles II, rather than the Calvinist executioner of his father, who issued the founding charter for the greatest scientific society in Europe. It would be hard to imagine a more humanistic manifesto than that in which the Royal Society announced its own ideals. Conversely, Thomas Jefferson, McLuhan's paragon of Ciceronian humanism, was scarcely inhibited by the identity thus assigned to him from "extracting the horsepower from the horse." As he wrote to George Fleming on December 29, 1815, "I had a fixed break to be moved by the gate of my sawmill, which broke and beat at the rate of two hundred pounds a day. But the inconveniences of interrupting that, induced me to try the power of a horse, and I have found it to answer perfectly. . . . I expect that a single horse will do the breaking and beating of ten men."[13]

3. In opposition to the humanist strain, McLuhan recognizes a so-called dialectical tradition initiated by Socrates in his quarrel with the Sophists. Even if one could accept the suggestion that this tradition was continuous, most of the facts contradict the assertion that it

[13] H. A. Washington, ed., *The Writings of Thomas Jefferson* (Washington, D.C.: Taylor and Maury, 1853–1854), VI, 504.

was the stream that nourished scientific development. In their separate ways both Plato and Aristotle inhibited the growth of science for more than a thousand years.

The monolithic mysticism of Plato paralyzed empirical inquiry by inviting men to neglect the appearance of physical reality in favor of the pristine Ideals that lurked beneath the surface. It would be hard to imagine an attitude that was more patently hostile to the pursuit of experimental science.

As for Aristotle, it is generally agreed that natural knowledge was almost entirely stultified by pedantic adherence to his system of inquiry.

McLuhan is certainly correct to associate the dialectical tradition with the name of Aristotle: this ancient Greek example was followed with great enthusiasm by the scholars of the Middle Ages, and the tradition of dispute that resulted yielded an extremely narrow form of intellectual specialism. But McLuhan is wrong to suppose that this specialism led to the development of science and technology. It is in fact impossible to imagine how it could have done so. For logic as such is epistemologically neutral. Being a deductive system, it can neither create nor destroy intellectual matter. The conclusions that it yields are already implied in the premises that are submitted to it. All that logic can do is to demonstrate the inevitable entailments of certain given propositions. If these propositions are corrupt, the conclusions based upon them will be corrupt also. If they are sterile the conclusions will be too. Logic, in other words, is a strictly tautologous enterprise, and it will only deliver new truths when fed with propositions that are based on factual observations. The machinery may be artfully redesigned so that it moves faster, but this will have no effect on the quality of the product that appears at the other end.

Ramus's simplification of many of Aristotle's more baroque categories is a case in point, but because he made no practical effort to improve the factual input, his streamlined machinery continued to deliver casuistical verbiage.

So that while McLuhan is perfectly right to point out that the New England universities of the seventeenth century inherited the reforms of Ramus, he is wrong to suggest that in doing so they confirmed an inclination toward scientific specialism. Sequestered on the shore of an uncivilized wilderness, the Ramistic academies of Harvard and Yale perpetuated the sterile logic-chopping of the Sorbonne and thereby exempted New England for at least a century from any significant part in the scientific revolution. It was only in the *humanistic* atmosphere of courtly Europe that empirical inquiry could breathe and grow.

The problem of the divergent fates of North and South that plays so central a part in McLuhan's early thought must therefore be reformulated. For if slavish adherence to logic, Ramistic or otherwise, inhibits rather than encourages the growth of science and technology, we must ask ourselves how the American North eventually achieved its vast industrial supremacy in spite of such a paralyzing inheritance. Conversely, why did the South lag so far behind in technological achievement, seeing that, as McLuhan insists, this region of America inherited the mainstream of humanism's facilitating tradition?

The answer to these questions lies in the investigation of social, economic, and demographic factors that have been conspicuously ignored by McLuhan in his enthusiasm to advertise the continuity of some utterly dubious struggle between the head and the heart.

The specialized patterns of Atlantic trade, for example, threw peculiar strains upon the economy of the North; and this was coupled with the fact that the vast influx of nineteenth-century European immigrants reorganized the social necessities of that region in such a way that technological opportunism was vigorously encouraged. Conversely, the aristocratic humanism of the Old South, insofar as it existed at all, was never concentrated or coherent enough to overcome the technological inertia that infects any society that depends upon cash crops and slave labor. Far from being the stable civic paradise painted by McLuhan, the Old South was a caldron of rampant rural individualism. It was restless, plural, and, above all, thinly settled. The volatile expansion of its population prevented that steady consolidation of shared human interests so essential to the growth of organized knowledge. If the South remained technologically backward it was not, as McLuhan implies, because it was *too* civilized, but, more direly, because it was not civilized *enough*.

From McLuhan's point of view an awkward contradiction arises immediately one turns his thesis upside down like this, thereby identifying the growth of technology with the humanistic tradition. For, in his eyes, it would seem incredible that a tradition that put such an eloquent emphasis on integral civic morality should yield to the dehumanized excesses of modern technology. What possible connection could there be between the encyclopedic decorum of Cicero, More, and Erasmus and the desolate specialized individualism of our modern industrial culture?

The question is not quite so paradoxical as it seems. If the lines of historical transmission were as straight as McLuhan suggests, he would of course be justified in being puzzled. But social development is much more complicated than that. No man can tell how subsequent generations will exploit and transform his ideas. No doubt Robert Boyle would have disowned the Satanic mills whose steam engines embodied the functional application of his own gas laws. But simply because the society that grew up around such establishments became corrupt, there is no reason to suppose that Boyle's own vision was infected with the seeds of spiritual decay. The fate of ideas and inventions is determined by the character of social institutions that choose to exploit them, and not by some hypothetical spiritual flaw ingrained in the imagination that produced the original invention.

The point is that McLuhan's historical enterprise is not really a descriptive one at all. It is a system of moral values in accordance with which he has rewritten history so as to make it embody the continuing story of an assault on these values. Far from recognizing an ancient quarrel in modern America he has paraphrased history in order to identify a modern quarrel in antiquity. Which might be legitimate if only one were sure that this modern quarrel had any real existence outside McLuhan's own somewhat schismatic imagination. As it is, however, the modern quarrel is largely created by a Manichaean view of the human personality, according to which the profane thrust of rational positivism is forever at odds with the prudent initiatives of heartfelt moral intelligence. In the light of such a clear-cut division it is of course easy to go back over the course of history and rearrange its component details until they fit. But in doing so the accumulated records of human development are made to degenerate into a sort of Rorschach blot into which the writer can project almost any shape he wants. Thus McLuhan, in spite of his contempt for so-called linear explanations, has been so hypnotized by his simple dualism that, in searching for its historical origins, he has automatically lapsed into a dramatic form of linearity himself.

The Single Point of View

● ● ●

iii

Up to the middle 1940s, McLuhan seems to have stagnated in a well-recognized form of cultural nostalgia. The familiar themes of conservative agrarianism repeat themselves like a monotonous fugue in the essays he published during the 1940s. When he was not celebrating the virtues of the Old South he was acting as critical spokesman on behalf of such writers as Joyce, Eliot, Pound, and Lewis—men who also found themselves painfully at odds with the profane democratic rationalism of modern life. Witness for instance this passage from his long article on Wyndham Lewis:

> The life of free intelligence has never, in the Western World, encountered such anonymous and universal hostility before. To read the "pamphlets" of Lewis is to become aware not

only of the scope of the forces arrayed against reason and art, but it is to have anatomized before one's eyes every segment of the contemporary scene of glamorized commerce and advertising, and, above all, of the bogus science, philosophy, art and literature which has been the main instrument in producing the universal stupefaction.

Lewis confronts modern society with the trained eye of a painter to whom the cut of every garment, every gesture, every contour is a richly expressive language. However, the modern man has long lost the use of his eyes. He only has ears and those for the Napoleonic and romantic thunder of Beethoven, the turgid and dionysiac megalomania of Wagner, the erotic day-dreaming of Tschaikowsky, or the tom-tom and African bottom-wagging of swing calling to rut. With Dr. Coué-like repetition we hear on every hand: "This isn't a war, it's a revolution." "We live in an age of transition." "Things will be different after this war." "This won't be the last war." Whether spoken by the responsible or the moronic, these remarks, and countless others like them, have no meaning. They are spoken in a trance of inattention while the reason is in permanent abeyance. They are typical of men who no longer understand the world they have made and which, as robots, they operate day by day.[1]

From now on McLuhan could easily have retired into the irritable solitude that often awaits nostalgic reactionaries of this sort. However, far from slipping into the obvious forms of splenetic irrelevance, he underwent a large-scale change of critical accent during the late 1940s, and it is now rather hard to reconcile the high patrician anguish of the St. Louis period with the euphoric acceptance that marks his work today.

---

[1] "Wyndham Lewis: Lemuel in Lilliput," p. 60.

Yet the change in attitudes is more apparent than real. By adopting a stance of artful detachment and by heaping contempt on all those who let their values show, McLuhan has managed to sponsor all his original preferences under the disguise of someone who has achieved a superlative freedom from "the single point of view."

He acquired this strategic tranquillity partly as a result of studying the life and work of Edgar Allan Poe. In 1944 he published an article whose main purpose was to locate Poe in the Southern tradition of chivalrous humanism:

> I propose [he explained] to suggest how Poe's achievements are to be understood in the light of a great tradition of life and letters which he derived from the South of his day. This tradition has been a continuous force in European law, letters, and politics from the time of the Greek sophists. It is most conveniently referred to as the Ciceronian ideal, since Cicero gave it to St. Augustine and St. Jerome, who in turn saw to it that it has never ceased to influence Western society. The Ciceronian ideal as expressed in the "De Oratore" or in St. Augustine's "De Doctrina Christiana" is the ideal of rational man reaching his noblest attainment in the expression of an eloquent wisdom.[2]

By fixing Poe within this admired tradition it might seem that McLuhan had merely added another name to the ranks of those who found themselves in futile opposition to modern life. But, according to McLuhan, Poe had derived from this embattled tradition a critical strategy that equipped him to *survive*, and not merely to deplore, the assaults of modern vulgarity. For, as Baude-

[2] "Edgar Poe's Tradition," p. 25.

laire recognized, Poe was the prototype of the aristocratic dandy—the original fastidious *flâneur* behind whose mask of ironic indifference the threatened values of old-fashioned humanism survived intact. To McLuhan, "Poe cannot be understood apart from the great Byronic tradition (which extends at least back to Cervantes) of the aristocratic rebel fighting for human values in a sub-human chaos of indiscriminate appetite."

In addition to the suggestive tactics offered by his life, Poe wrote a famous story that provided McLuhan with a highly specific metaphor of moral survival—a metaphor that emphasized the advantages to be gained from detachment. In *A Descent into the Maelstrom* Poe tells of a sailor who finds himself swirling to destruction on the walls of a notorious whirlpool. At first he is naturally overcome with panic and despair. Soon, however, his scientific curiosity gets the better of his fear, and he notices that by studying the behavior of the debris floating on the surface of the lethal current he can actually predict the action of the maelstrom. Instead of exhausting himself by fighting the irresistible force of the water he decides to surrender, and before long he is swept from the turmoil unscathed.

This simple story provided McLuhan with a vivid working model for survival. The whirlpool is the social chaos produced by man's technical ingenuity. The power of this artificial maelstrom is by now so enormous that it is hopeless to try to swim against it. If, however, like Poe's sailor, the anguished moralist can suspend his panic and observe rather than deplore the profane swirl, he will conserve his energy and eventually learn to cooperate to his own advantage. McLuhan therefore repudiated indignation in favor of amused vigilance. As he wrote later in the preface of *The Mechanical Bride*:

It was this amusement born of his rational detachment as a spectator of his own situation that gave him the thread which led him out of the Labyrinth. And it is in the same spirit that this book is offered as an amusement. Many who are accustomed to the note of moral indignation will mistake this amusement for mere indifference. But the time for anger and protest is in the early stages of a new process. The present stage is extremely advanced. Moreover, it is full, not only of destructiveness but also of promises of rich new developments to which moral indignation is a very poor guide.[3]

The publication in 1951 of *The Mechanical Bride* marked McLuhan's own descent into the maelstrom. In this remarkable volume, little recognized when it first appeared, he compiled a cyclorama of commercial exhibits taken from the mass media and then "set the reader at the center of this revolving picture . . . where he may (like Poe's sailor) observe the action."

But *The Mechanical Bride* is not just a merry-go-round of specimens taken from the mass media. There would have been no point in simply re-creating a scale model of the maelstrom, since the modern public had already lived at the center of the real one for more than sixty years without having availed itself of the opportunity for observing its dire effects. McLuhan therefore wrote a detailed running commentary, in the course of which he tried to release "the intelligible meaning of the various exhibits," hoping thereby, like a psychoanalyst, to release his readers from their slavery to them. For McLuhan identified the various specimens as synthetic dreams meeting "a somnambulist public that accepts them un-

---

[3] *The Mechanical Bride*, p. v.

critically. Otherwise how explain the absence of reaction in the name of the human dignity they destroy?"

The dream, as Freud realized, is a subtly dramatized fulfillment of desires that society forbids the individual to gratify. These appetites, however, can never be destroyed. Sublimated into fantasy, they retain and even redouble their strength, and are only prevented from disturbing consciousness by discharging themselves in the altered form of dreams.

Freud realized that the manifest content of the dream gave no immediate clue to the motives that created it. The unconscious dramatizes its frustrations in code in order that the conscious mind may retain its complacent belief that it has actually abolished the appetites that society has told it to repudiate. When the waking subject recalls his dream, he is therefore often puzzled by its bizarre irrelevance, unaware that he has just performed, in disguise as it were, a shadow version of the very acts that society has prohibited.

According to McLuhan the advertisement, the comic strip, and the movie have many important features in common with the dream. They also work their various effects by concealing their correspondence with the secret motives of the unconscious mind.

How, he asks, is this artful correspondence achieved? By systematic research into the dynamics of human motive; and by translating the results into cunningly contrived programs of entertainment and persuasion. In other words, by kidnapping the products of self-knowledge and putting them to work in the service of deliberate control. This, by McLuhan's account, is where humanity has been betrayed by its own technical ingenuity. Time was when "the know-how of the twelfth century was dedicated to an all-inclusive knowledge of human and divine ends. The secularization of this system has meant the adaptation of techniques not for knowledge but control."

As usual McLuhan is remarkably confident and definitive in dating these supposedly critical events in cultural history. Nevertheless he *is* correct in recognizing that psychological knowledge may be exploited in two entirely different ways.

For the pious moralist, self-knowledge is an end in itself—"the desire and pursuit of the whole." And if, as Augustine recognized, the mind is vaster than most of its owners realize, there are within each of us vast tracts of psychic territory awaiting ethical colonization. The more we know about this region, the better we are able to direct our behavior toward decent ends. Insofar as we are dictated by unconscious motives, we are to some extent automata. By enlarging the scope of self-knowledge we reduce the number of actions that are automatic and increase those that are deliberate. Since ethics only deals with actions that are deliberate, our moral status is magnified with each increment in self-knowledge.

The same knowledge may, however, be used to subvert rather than assist moral freedom. That is to say, our unconscious mind may be commandeered by experts who have specialized knowledge of its susceptibilities, and used by them to dictate our behavior without our knowing consent. How could such a thing happen? How could we be prompted to act against our choice without immediately knowing that we had been interfered with? Because, as Freud discovered, a certain proportion of our behavior is already dictated by urges that we neither recognize nor control. If the unconscious can deliver its motives into consciousness in such a form that the individual acts upon them as if they were undertaken of his own free will, it is theoretically possible for someone with expert knowledge of the mind to program the unconscious in order to influence the behavior of a given subject without his necessarily feeling that he has been constrained in any way.

This is just what McLuhan believes has happened. By creating an elite class of psychological technicians we have inadvertently sold the franchise to our own unconscious.

> Striving constantly . . . to watch, anticipate, and control events on the inner, invisible stage of the collective dream, the ad agencies and Hollywood turn themselves unwittingly into a sort of collective novelist, whose characters, imagery, and situations are an intimate revelation of the passions of the age. But this huge collective novel can be read only by someone trained to use his eyes and ears, and in detachment from the visceral riot that this sensational fare tends to produce. The reader has to be a second Ulysses in order to withstand the siren onslaught. Or, to vary the image, the uncritical reader of this collective novel is like the person who looked directly at the face of Medusa without the mirror of conscious reflection. He stands in danger of being frozen into a helpless robot. Without the mirror of the mind, nobody can live a human life in the face of our present mechanized dream.[4]

The function of *The Mechanical Bride* therefore is the restoration of vigilance. By using multiple cross references in literature, anthropology, and social psychology

[4] *Ibid.*, p. 97.

McLuhan forces his audience to recognize the way in which their various desires have been appropriated to commercial ends.

For example, he quotes an advertisement for a diesel engine which creates a persuasive elision between the idea of mechanical power and the virile strength of a prize fighter:

RINGSIDE SEAT FOR A BATTLE ROYAL!

Correct Lubrication Fights for You Inside Your Diesel and Throughout Your Plant!
You're in the front row, looking at a terrific battle inside a big Diesel engine . . .
This battle royal is typical of similar battles going on constantly inside all the machines in your plant.

The man who wrote the above copy had a natural feeling for the relations between the prize fight and heavy industry. The century of spectacular prize fighting which lies behind us coincides with the era of the maulers and bruisers of industry. A more subtle age of bureaucratic and monopolistic business enterprise calls for the more complex sport of "push-button football." Modern football would have bored to death the tycoons of yesteryear, because they would have found in it none of the dramatization of their own lives. Sport is a kind of magic or ritual, varying with the changing character of the dominant classes. And it embodies in a symbolic way the drives and tensions of a society.[5]

McLuhan employs the same technique when examining the popular heroes of American comics. Dagwood, in the Blondie strip, for instance, is

"the American way of life." But Chick Young's strip seems to be assured of survival into a world which

5 *Ibid.*, p. 123.

will be as alien to it as it already is to McManus's Jiggs. Those who grew up with Dagwood will, like those who grew up with Jiggs, insist on growing old with him. For many millions on this continent Jiggs and Dagwood are fixed points of geniality, beacons of orientation, amid flux and stress. They represent a new kind of entertainment, a sort of magically recurrent daily ritual which now exerts on the spontaneous popular feelings a rhythmic reassurance that does substitute service, as it were, for the old popular experience of the recurrence of the seasons.[6]

McLuhan was not the first to make this sort of analysis of modern mass culture. George Orwell, Wyndham Lewis, and other writers had already made distinctive contributions to our understanding of it. Wyndham Lewis had recognized the drowsing automatism of modern man, and in the scorching polemic of *Time and Western Man* he also identified the dismal syntax of the advertisement. Orwell had recognized the elementary psychology that lay underneath the blood-and-thunder stories in boys' magazines; and in the famous essay on seaside postcards, he benevolently identified the popular expression of what he calls "the unofficial self." In the same vein, the American critic Robert Warshow exposed the characteristic appeal of the gangster movie, showing for instance how the gangster's death "pays for our fantasies, releasing us momentarily both from the content of success which he denies by caricaturing it, and from the need to succeed, which he shows to be dangerous." There are many other examples of such cultural "psychoanalysis"; so that in one respect at least McLuhan was contributing to a well-developed form of cultural criticism.

[6] *Ibid.*, p. 69.

But McLuhan distinguishes himself from most of the other critics of mass culture in recognizing that "it is full, not only of destructiveness but also of promises of rich new developments to which moral indignation is a poor guide." This unexpected switch from resignation to frank optimism was accomplished by making a careful and previously overlooked distinction between the form and the content of the material under consideration. While he loudly denounced the *matter* of advertisements and newspaper cartoons, he identified certain characteristics of form and structure whereby these otherwise deplorable creations were closely related to all that he thought best and most regenerative in avant-garde poetry and painting.

For instance, in a Berkshire stocking advertisement, where an effort has been made to sell the product by appealing to sexual instinct, the copywriter has bypassed the prudish vigilance of the conscious mind by omitting the obvious syntactical connections between the image of a rearing stallion and that of the demure lady drawn alongside: "Juxtaposition of items permits the advertiser to 'say,' by methods which *Time* has used to great effect, what could never pass the censor of consciousness. A most necessary contrast to 'raging animality' is that a girl should appear gentle, refined, aloof, and innocent. It's her innocence, her obvious 'class' that's terrific, because dramatically opposed to the suggestion of brutal violation."[7]

The unconscious mind, primitive and immediate in its action, supplies the missing connections and understands, in a way that the conscious mind finds difficult, that there can be "symbolic unity amongst the most di-

[7] *Ibid.*, p. 81.

verse and externally unconnected facts and situations."
While McLuhan correctly bemoans the fact that human
susceptibilities should be callously exploited in this manner, he celebrates the triumph of a technique that is
otherwise honorably used by modern poets and painters.

For practitioners of an enterprise that is widely despised by artists and intellectuals, it gave an enormous
boost to self-esteem to have their work identified, even
at a debased level, with the exalted initiatives of Picasso.
It is hardly surprising that Madison Avenue pays such
extravagant respect to McLuhan. Copywriters and other
exponents of the mass media have grown increasingly
sensitive to liberal and radical criticism. Many of these
men are university graduates and as such are seriously
embarrassed to find themselves practicing an art they
have been taught as students to suspect. It is easy to
imagine their pleasure, therefore, on discovering a university professor who recognizes, in their joint undertak-
ing, not merely a creative element but a creative element
that represents one of the "most hopeful developments in
thought and feeling."

What McLuhan claimed to have identified in the advertisement was an idiom that poets and writers of the
modern movement had also recognized in the myth, the
fairy tale, and the dream; that is to say a quality of immediate allusive thought where ideas and images are free
to imply one another without formal connections. In the
fairy tale, for instance, as Chesterton pointed out, the
ordinary laws of cause are suspended in favor of magical
imperatives. "In the fairy tale an incomprehensible hap-
piness rests upon an incomprehensible condition. A box
is opened, and all evils fly out. A word is forgotten, and
cities perish. A lamp is lit, and love flies away. A flower

is plucked, and human lives are forfeited. An apple is eaten, and the hope of God is gone."[8]

According to McLuhan, literacy and logic have curtailed this capacity for creating allusive cross reference and, as a result, we have violated the integral simultaneity of primitive experience. Ideas have been gradually shorn of their imaginative "polyvalence" so that instead of being able to associate with one another in large suggestive clusters they are forced to link up in simple disciplined succession. For all the practical advantages that might have been gained from such a discipline, it has in the long run, says McLuhan, imposed a "spurious intelligibility" upon our experience and lost us the priceless inheritance of total awareness.

McLuhan himself points out that he was by no means the first to notice that the mass media contained features that usefully reverted to those of prelogical thought:

> The French symbolists, followed by James Joyce in *Ulysses*, saw that there was a new art form of universal scope present in the technical layout of the modern newspaper. Here is a major instance of how a by-product of industrial imagination, a genuine agency of contemporary folk-lore, led to radical artistic developments. To the alerted eye, the front page of a newspaper is a superficial chaos which can lead the mind to attend to cosmic harmonies of a very high order. Yet when these harmonies are more sharply stylized by a Picasso or a Joyce, they seem to give offence to the very people who should appreciate them most. But that is a separate story.[9]

[8] G. K. Chesterton, *Orthodoxy* (London: John Lane, Bodley Head, 1909), p. 98.
[9] *The Mechanical Bride*, p. 4.

Moral indignation, as McLuhan himself emphasizes, would be a poor guide to arriving at such perceptions. However, he has been able to achieve his own freedom from such indignation only by ignoring the content of the mass media and by concentrating on their abstract form instead. In other words, in *The Mechanical Bride* we can see a primitive overture to his subsequent interest in the Medium at the expense of the Message.

One cannot help being disturbed by the abdication of political intelligence implied in such an attitude. It may well be the case that the techniques employed by copywriters have a great deal in common with those used by avant-garde artists. However, it is one thing to identify such a similarity; it is another thing to celebrate it. By rejoicing in the fact that a Berkshire stocking advertisement shares structural features with a Picasso, we are distracted from the urgent need to criticize the economic institutions that resort to such techniques in their effort to get us to buy. However, the various procedures that one might use for such criticism are the very ones that McLuhan despises—"morbid symptoms whose impulses are neither social nor rational, but technological derivatives."

The emphasis upon structural analysis that sets *The Mechanical Bride* apart from most of the other commentaries on the mass media puts McLuhan in line with a critical tradition that found its most eloquent exponent in the Swiss art historian Heinrich Wölfflin. Wölfflin, a student of Jakob Burckhardt, succeeded in creating a method of pictorial analysis that largely ignored the emotional tone and narrative content of the paintings under consideration. He was able to distinguish national and epochal differences simply by looking at the way in which various artists handled the structure of pictorial space. For instance, in distinguishing between the "classic" art of the cinquecento and the "baroque" art of the seicento Wölfflin suggested a set of criteria all of which are completely independent of narrative or emotional content.

Wölfflin's student Siegfried Giedion developed this tradition of formal analysis. In the influential lectures that he delivered at Harvard in 1941 and later published as *Space, Time and Architecture*, he combined Wölfflin's technique of pictorial analysis with a concern for the destiny of modern culture—anticipating, almost word for word, the sense of crisis that prompted McLuhan to write *The Mechanical Bride*. *Space, Time and Architecture* is intended for "those who are alarmed by the present state of our culture and anxious to find a way out of the apparent chaos of its contradictory tendencies." Like Poe's sailor, Giedion suggests that although the maelstrom *appears* chaotic, it fundamentally obeys simple laws that will be revealed by calm scrutiny: "I have attempted to establish, both by argument and by objective evidence, that in spite of the seeming confusion there is nevertheless a true, if hidden, unity, a secret synthesis, in our present civilization. To point out *why* this synthesis has *not* become *a conscious and active reality* has been one of my chief aims."[10]

Anticipating the technique of *The Mechanical Bride* by nearly a decade, Giedion repudiated an encyclopedic study of art history and chose to reveal the truth in terms of a few well-chosen exhibits. "*History*," he affirms, "*is not a compilation of facts, but an insight into a moving process of life.* Moreover, such insight is obtained not

[10] Siegfried Giedion, *Space, Time and Architecture* (Cambridge, Mass.: Harvard University Press, 1941), p. v.

by the exclusive use of the panoramic survey, the bird's-eye view, but by isolating and examining certain specific events intensively, penetrating and exploring them in the manner of the close-up. This procedure makes it possible to evaluate a culture from within as well as from without."[11]

The central thesis of Giedion's intriguing and paradoxical book is that until the start of the twentieth century painters and artists struggled to resolve the various problems of representation in spatial terms that were dictated by the Renaissance discovery of perspective:

> In linear "perspective"—etymologically "clear-seeing"—objects are depicted upon a plane surface in conformity with the way they are seen, without reference to their absolute shapes or relations. The whole picture or design is calculated to be valid for one station or observation point only. To the fifteenth century the principle of perspective came as a complete revolution, involving an extreme and violent break with the medieval conception of space, and with the flat, floating arrangements which were its artistic expression.
>
> With the invention of perspective the modern notion of individualism found its artistic counterpart. Every element in a perspective representation is related to the unique point of view of the individual spectator.[12]

The parallel between this statement and McLuhan's own peculiar horror of the "single point of view" is too obvious to need further elaboration.

According to Giedion the collective discovery of cubism subverted the monotonous decorum of Renaissance

[11] *Ibid.*
[12] *Ibid.*, p. 31.

perspective, usurped the authority of the "single point of view," and gave simultaneous expression to all aspects of a given object. McLuhan has consistently developed Giedion's theme throughout his later writing, especially in seeing that the same structural revolution has also occurred in literature. In a piece on Tennyson, he wrote:

> The principal innovation was that of *le paysage interieur* or the psychological landscape. This landscape, by means of discontinuity, which was first developed in picturesque painting, effected the apposition of widely diverse objects as a means of establishing what Mr. Eliot has called "an objective correlative" for a state of mind. The openings of "Prufrock," "Gerontion" and *The Waste Land* illustrate Mr. Eliot's growth in the adaptation of this technique, as he passed from the influence of Laforgue to that of Rimbaud, from personal to impersonal manipulation of experience. Whereas in external landscape diverse things lie side by side, so in psychological landscape the juxtaposition of various things and experiences becomes a precise musical means of orchestrating that which could never be rendered by systematic discourse. Landscape is the means of presenting, without the copula of logical enunciation, experiences which are united in existence but not in conceptual thought. Syntax becomes music, as in Tennyson's "Mariana."[13]

In his studies of European literature McLuhan has consistently favored those writers who could reproduce the imaginative discontinuities of prelogical thought. Thomas Nashe, for instance—the subject of McLuhan's Cambridge Ph.D. thesis—is praised for the way in which

[13] "Tennyson and Picturesque Poetry," pp. 270–71.

his "polyphonic prose offends lineal decorum." The same masterful neglect of "logical copulae" drew him to Joyce, especially for the way in which Joyce was able to "reacquire proprietorship of the human past" by the juxtaposition of more than one period of time within the same frame of literary reference: "In the same way *Ulysses* is 1904 A.D. but also 800 B.C. And the continuous parallel between ancient and modern provides a 'cubist' rather than a linear perspective. It is a world of a 'timeless present' such as we meet in the order of objections in a Thomistic article, but also typical of the nonperspective discontinuities of medieval art in general. History is abolished not by being disowned but by becoming present."[14]

According to McLuhan, formal literacy tends to "shun these nets of analogies" and, by reducing them to linear statements, severs our sacred continuity with human tradition. However, by means of the pun, the paradox, and the myth, these nourishing connections can soon be re-established. The puns in *Finnegans Wake* are to McLuhan "a technique for revealing this submerged drama of language, and Joyce relied on the quirks, 'slips', and freaks of ordinary discourse to evoke the fullness of existence in speech. All his life he played the sleuth with words, shadowing them and waiting confidently for some unexpected situation to reveal their hidden signatures and powers."[15]

Small wonder then that McLuhan found so much to admire in Chesterton; and it is interesting to note that when in 1947 Hugh Kenner published his short study *Paradox in Chesterton* McLuhan supplied the introduc-

[14] "James Joyce: Trivial and Quadrivial," p. 95.
[15] *Ibid.*, p. 89.

tion. This extract from Kenner's essay summarizes McLuhan's own views on the matter:

> Verbal paradox is the artist's prerogative, because the artist with a specific aim to accomplish uses it knowingly to persuade, while anyone else may avoid it if he chooses. Its method is to exploit the double senses analogically possessed by single words; the principle, in other words, is always, in some form or other, the pun, and by way of the pun Chesterton is heir to a long tradition; for to perceive puns is ultimately to perceive a totality of words and things and feelings analogically. His use of the verbal paradox is always intricate and multiple, because to use it simply, to correct on one page and to startle on another, is to assume that the reader is sometimes wholly wrong and at other times wholly asleep.[16]

It is important to recognize at this point that while McLuhan continued to sponsor the spiritual dichotomy that he had already identified in the "Ancient Quarrel," he was now determined to characterize the two halves of the quarrel with specific reference to the ways in which they each handled the concepts of space and time.

Heartfelt humanistic thought, with its roots in the preliterate imagination, ignored the formal constraint of Euclidean space, abolished the conventional intervals between disparate concepts, and reconstructed a timeless space within which ideas were free to associate on the basis of their mutual analogical affinities. Within this psychologically permissive universe the imagination was freed at last to obtain deep spiritual enlightenment from, in the words of Max Ernst, the "fortuitous encounters

[16] Hugh Kenner, *Paradox in Chesterton* (New York: Sheed & Ward, 1947), p. 57.

upon a non-suitable plane of two mutually distant real-
ities."

Formal discourse, on the other hand, inherited from
the Socratics and eagerly developed finally by the tech-
nical-scientific specialists, celebrated the conceptual supremacy of explicit logical connections. Arranging its
subject matter within the decorous vistas of three-
dimensional space, it took care to regulate its descriptions
of reality in accordance with the laws of cause and effect.
McLuhan clearly favored the former regime, insisting
that the integral moral sense of the ancient humanist
could flourish only within the analogical networks of the
timeless present. No matter how vast the three-dimensional space of modern scientific determinism, there was
still no room in it for the unpredictable initiatives of
human love and imagination.

By the early 1950s, then, McLuhan's Procrustean enthusiasm had produced a set of spiritual dichotomies all
of which are metaphorical counterparts of one another
(see below). Although McLuhan had identified these
various schisms with great historical confidence, he
had not yet formulated a psychological theory that would
explain why they existed in the first place. Just as Darwin
had to postpone his theory of natural selection until he
had read Malthus's *Essay on Population*, so McLuhan
was forced to delay his famous typographic hypothesis
until he had come into contact with the Canadian economic historian Harold Adams Innis.

1. Head   Heart
2. Reason   Imagination
3. Abstract logic   Concrete imaginative
                       intuition

4. Syllogisms and entailments	Puns, paradoxes, metaphors
5. Formal linear arguments with concepts related to one another in terms of explicit logical connections	Imaginative affinities with concepts related to one another in terms of their analogical overlaps
6. "Exterior" landscape with all objects related to one another according to the laws of perspective	"Interior" landscape with scenes and objects torn out of their spatio-temporal context and rearranged next to one another without logical copulae
7. Renaissance perspective with a single "point of view"	Cubist "perspective" with all aspects depicted within a single frame
8. Linear sequential thought	Condensed metaphorical simultaneity
9. Euclid	Einstein
10. Secular three-dimensional space within which all change is dictated by laws of cause and effect	Sacred "time" without tenses. Change is illusory
11. Science with knowledge as control	Religion with knowledge as piety
12. Industry	Agriculture
13. Grammarians	Sophists
14. Specialized logical technology	Eloquent "encyclopedic" humanism
15. Secular mercantile bourgeoisie	Pious Cavalier gentry
16. American North	American South

The lesson that McLuhan drew from Innis was utterly deterministic, and its explanation of the cultural schisms that he had already recognized squares rather uneasily with his avowed contempt for arguments based on linear causality. Innis was a graduate of the University of Chicago and an eloquent advocate of the technological determinism he had learned there from Robert Ezra Park, who maintained that technological devices, having changed men's habits, "in doing so . . . have necessarily modified the structure and functions of society. . . . From this point of view it seems that every technical device, from the wheelbarrow to the aeroplane, in so far as it provided a new and more effective means of locomotion, has, or should have, marked an epoch in society."[17]

Innis developed this deterministic theme in a remarkable little volume published in 1950, in which he—like Park (and Siegfried Giedion)—argued that the main force of social change, which included alterations in cultural sensibility, was to be found in the various revolutions that had taken place in technology, especially in the technology of communications.

In his opinion, traditional social analysis had somewhat misidentified the sources of cultural differentiation. For while he agreed that the character of society is largely determined by the wisdom and knowledge shared by its individual members, he insisted that both the origins and the social effects of such knowledge are determined as much by the physical peculiarities of the media through which they are transmitted as by any of the actual propositions which they comprise.

In the developing history of communications, Innis identified certain crucial characteristics of media, paying

[17] Robert Ezra Park, *Society* (Glencoe, Ill.: Free Press, 1955).

special attention to their respective permanence and portability. The most dramatic distinction he found is the one that exists between writing and speaking. Theoretically the human voice will transmit an infinite variety of information, but certain constraints are placed upon this variety by the peculiar physical properties of sound.

1. *Sound can travel only over relatively short distances*, so that although the individual members of an oral society are more or less free to move as they wish, they will naturally tend to gravitate toward a point at which the largest number of oral exchanges can be overheard. Moving outward from this conversationally dense center, oral exchanges become thinner and thinner and finally vanish altogether. The sense of social space therefore is vaguely defined by the fluid contours of collective earshot. Beyond this amoeboid boundary the world at large becomes a silent, mysterious void into which the collective imagination tends to project all sorts of magic fantasy.

2. *Sound disperses even more rapidly in time than it does in space*, so that unless an utterance is preserved in the memory of an attentive audience it will be lost forever. Not that it survives in its original form even then; for memory is not a passive receptacle from which experiences may be retrieved just as they went in. It is an editorial ministry that reconstructs its past experience in accordance with the peculiar interests of the imagination. Therefore the past that an oral culture shapes for itself tells us more about the collective mentality of the group than it does about the historical reality to which its constituent memories supposedly refer.

Fictional though such a "past" may be, it looms larger in the social imagination than does the complementary image of geographical space. This is presumably what Innis means when he refers to oral societies as being "time-bound." Grouped around the narrow wellhead of collective earshot, such communities more or less disregard the geographical territory beyond their conversational centers and affirm their sense of group identity with special reference to the authority of an imaginatively reconstructed normative past.

Moreover, without any collateral records against which to check such fictions, myth and history merge into one. The metaphorical idioms that characterize the imagination assume unrivaled supremacy over logico-empirical styles of thought; with the immediate result that the group realizes its own identity with more or less exclusive reference to sacred or religious standards of legitimacy.

Consider now, says Innis, what happens when writing is introduced, especially when committed to permanent portable media such as paper. Communications can now survive without distortion over space and time.

1. *Space.* Since orders and instructions can now arrive at remote destinations in exactly the same form that they were dispatched, a society that employs writing can maintain relatively complex political identity over wide geographical areas. Far-flung bureaucratic control becomes possible, with the result that the secular opportunities of the present begin to overwhelm the importance previously assigned to the normative past. The stage is set for profane acquisitive nationalism.

2. *Time.* The existence of objective historical records introduces the possibility of a critical scrutiny of inherited wisdom. The obedience previously accorded to certain charismatic sources of oral reminiscence gives way to individual judgment; with the result that the

imaginative integrity of the sacred past no longer exerts such a comprehensive hold upon the individual members of a literate community. Thought becomes piecemeal, empirical, and, above all, open to objective standards of judgment.

This brief summary of Innis's theory somewhat abuses the subtlety with which he himself approached the problem of the bias of communications. For he was careful not to segregate the effects of media too sharply, and took pains to show that the various tendencies that he identified overlapped and even blurred into one another. McLuhan, however, recognized a fundamental dualism that corroborated the distinction he had already identified independently. Here at last was a concrete technological explanation for the fatal division between the head and the heart.

Innis's theory was all the more attractive for the way in which it reflected a collateral distinction embodied in the linguistic theories of Benjamin Lee Whorf—theories that also placed a peculiar emphasis upon the way in which differences in communication imposed corresponding differences in world outlook. Whorf insisted, for example, as a result of his investigations of the Hopi language, that the subjective image of both physical and social reality was largely determined by the grammatical character of the language used to express it—an idea that had already been suggested by the linguist Edward Sapir.

Whorf noticed that the Hopi were curiously indifferent to mechanistic interpretations of nature, which are in turn so characteristic of modern Western culture. In *Language, Thought and Reality* he went on to show that this divergence could be explained with reference to the syntactical differences that existed between Hopi and Standard Average European:

> It . . . became evident that even the grammar of Hopi bore a relation to Hopi culture, and the grammar of European tongues to our own "Western" or "European" culture. And it appeared that the interrelation brought in those large subsummations of experience by language, such as our own terms "time," "space," "substance," and "matter." Since, with respect to the traits compared, there is little difference between English, French, German, or other European languages with the *possible* (but doubtful) exception of Balto-Slavic and non-Indo-European, I have lumped these languages into one group called SAE, or "Standard Average European."[18]

Although Innis seemed unaware of Whorf, and while Whorf himself made little or no reference to the effects of literacy, McLuhan sought to establish a theory that would bring both these authorities together and show that the bias of communications recognized by Innis was directly related to the linguistic relativity identified by Whorf. But to effect this marriage McLuhan found it necessary to elaborate a mediating hypothesis that translated both sets of ideas into the terms of general epistemology. In doing so he ventured well beyond the available facts, and fell into some dangerous logical pitfalls.

[18] Benjamin Lee Whorf, *Language, Thought and Reality*, ed. John B. Carroll (jointly published by Technology Press, MIT, Cambridge, Mass.; John Wiley, New York; and Chapman & Hall, London, 1956), p. 138.

Language, Literacy, and the Media

●

IV

To accommodate Whorf's and Innis's proposals within the more inclusive framework of the philosophy of mind, McLuhan found it necessary to elaborate a psychological theory that owes considerably more to the unacknowledged authority of St. Thomas Aquinas than it does to any of the scientific sources he openly refers to. McLuhan's theory places at the center of the human mind a psychic organ within which the five senses collaborate to provide a common ground of conscious experience.

Interpreted in a weak sense, this notion is no more than an inoffensive paraphrase of the self-evident proposition that human consciousness comprises, in Bradley's phrase, an uncounted plural whole. But McLuhan makes a questionable advance upon this simple truism by asserting that the acknowledged plurality of sensory experience is mediated by a psychic structure whose composition is characterized by an arithmetical ratio, and that this ratio governs the quantitative representation in consciousness of each of the five senses. The existence of such a ratio confers a binding numerical reciprocity upon the five respective quanta of physical sensation in such a way that increases in the contribution made by any one of them automatically leads to a proportional shrinkage in each of the other four—and vice versa.

Now according to McLuhan the most effective single method of introducing such shifts in differential emphasis is to reinforce the function of one sense organ through the aid of an artificial device applied to it. Anything, for example, that extends the range and sensitivity of the eyes will immediately "step up the intensity of vision," thereby causing a reciprocal extinction in the sense of hearing—not to mention the other three senses. Any individual who has been systematically exposed to such partial assistance will suffer a permanent change in his capacity to comprehend the full variety of the world around him.

To the average layman, this scheme may seem more impressive than it really is. For unfortunately the use of high-sounding quantitative terms—ratio, bias, and sensory mix—is no guarantee of the scientific credibility of a scheme that makes use of such notions. Before the concepts of "ratio" and "bias" can be assigned any substantial meaning, there must be a clear statement that specifies the physical operations in which such terms are grounded. If not, the concepts remain vacuous and any theory based upon them falls to the ground.

How does McLuhan's basic assumption stand up in the light of such criticism? Not very well, I am afraid.

For when he refers to the "natural ratio" that prevails between the five senses he makes no effort to specify the units it comprises, and unless such a specification can be made the notion of "ratio" has no meaning. If, as McLuhan seems to suggest, the *sensus communis* is a sort of psychic receptacle, and if its sensory composition depends upon the relative intensities of the five streams of sensation that replenish it, it should be possible to specify the physical procedures by which these respective "intensities" are measured. Otherwise there is no firm ground from which to make the assertion that a given technique has stepped up "the intensity of vision."

As it is, McLuhan inadvertently makes it very difficult for himself to satisfy even this preliminary requirement, since he employs the concept of sensory intensity in a way that makes it categorically impossible to imagine the measuring procedures that might be relevant to it. He speaks, for instance, about print "stepping up the intensity of vision," which is not wrong exactly but meaningless. For vision is not the sort of "thing" to which the concept of intensity can be significantly applied. One may talk about the intensity of a visual *stimulus*—but it makes no sense to talk about the intensity of *vision*.

Let me illustrate this by a counterexample. The intensity of a spot of light can be immediately defined by giving the number of foot-candles in the incident source, or by reading off the figures on the scale of a galvanometer which has been inserted into the electric current that activates the light. Increases in the intensity of the *stimulus* can then be formally registered as a multiple of the units that have been chosen. Once this scale has been defined in terms of the measurements that give it meaning, it becomes perfectly reasonable to try and correlate the increase in stimulus intensity with, say, the number of nerve impulses generated at any given intensity. Both sets of measurements are conceptually legitimated by the fact that they are founded upon physical operations that can properly yield numbers. This does not, and indeed cannot, hold for "vision" as a whole. One might just as well try to measure the force of circumstance or the weight of grief.

Bearing these logical objections in mind, it is very hard to attach serious scientific significance to McLuhan's assertion that the *sensus communis* is compiled in accordance with a ratio that we disturb at our peril.

To be fair, however, there *is* a psychological context within which it is reasonable to speak of variations in sensory bias—and that of course is the context of human attention. Ordinary introspection tells us that we can sometimes attend to one sensory mode at the expense of all the others. If something captures our visual attention we become relatively inattentive to information coming in through the ear. A severe pain in the belly can often monopolize our attention to the complete exclusion of an otherwise interesting visual scene, but we do not think of such phenomena as constituting an assault upon the primitive ratio of the *sensus communis*. The act of paying attention, far from being a departure from some hypothetical norm of mental activity, is one of its customary variations in accordance with which that norm is actually defined. A mind that cannot shift its attention from one area of interest to another is damaged in some way.

Again, to be fair to McLuhan, I am sure that he would *not* regard such "normal" shifts of attention as being perilous assaults upon the integrity of the *sensus communis*. According to him, the real danger arises when

human beings start to rely upon *artificial* aids to perception; and he insists, for example, that instruments that
aid the eye freeze the attention in the visual mode. Now
although this claim is considerably more sophisticated
than the ones I have already criticized, it is riddled with
serious inconsistencies nevertheless. Basically, the same
objections apply to this suggestion as apply to the hypothetical claim that shifts in *natural* attention damage the
sensory integrity of the mind. Let me take this point in
some detail.

Consider the eye, for example. There is a limit upon
its powers of optical resolution, and the sensitivity of the
retina prevents it from working efficiently beyond certain
fixed values of light intensity. There are, however, a number of simple maneuvers by which the subject can overcome these limits, to a certain extent at least. Let me
take the natural ones first. In excessively bright light, for
example, the hand can be brought up to shade the eyes,
and when a distant object is beyond the powers of naked
resolution the subject is perfectly free to step up and look
closer. In both these cases the scope and the sensitivity of
the eye have been functionally extended beyond their
normal range, though in neither case has the *quantity of
vision* been increased. All that has happened is that
the area of the world within which the pre-existing capacity to switch visual attention is exercised has been
enlarged; and since this enlargement has taken place in
the external world, it is illogical to assert that a given
compartment of the mind has thereby been expanded.

The same principle applies to any artificial device that
extends the range or sensitivity of a given sense organ.
Lenses and electric lights, for instance, open up new
vistas for the naked eye. They extend the number of circumstances within which vision can operate, but multi-

plying the *options* of vision in this way does not magnify *vision* itself. For in the act of taking up any one of these new options, the eye must, by definition, momentarily neglect all the others. In order to take advantage of the visual opportunities offered by a microscope, for example, it is necessary for a moment to ignore the panorama outside the laboratory window. Looking down a microscope is indeed just another slightly more elaborate way of paying attention. The fact that it is accomplished with the aid of artificial lenses exerts no influence upon the faculty of vision as such.

In all fairness it is important to acknowledge a subtle qualification of this basic principle. If artificial aids to perception increase the number of circumstances within which the eye can operate, there is always the possibility that the *mental note* taken of such increased visual options may bias the central nervous system in favor of visual attention. Once the mind realizes that it has an extended visual field within which to exercise its choice of glance, it could, theoretically at least, bias its cognitive expectancy in such a way that it becomes relatively impervious to events that are trying to reach it through sensory channels not thus privileged.

There is, however, a logical circularity embedded in this proposal too, associated with the fact that it makes no sense to talk of *imposing* increased sensory options upon a subject. One can impose constraints but one cannot impose options. One can, for instance, rear a subject in the dark or fit him from birth with red goggles, and in doing so impose a serious constraint upon the variety of his visual experience; but if one takes a normal subject and offers him extra optical apparatus through the successive exploitation of which he can multiply the variety of his visual experiences, one has imposed nothing whatsoever; one has merely offered an increased range of visual options. The subject is free to take them up as, when, and if he chooses to. If he does take them up, he demonstrates in the act of doing so the very visual interest that McLuhan supposes to be the *consequence* of such artificial opportunities.

Presumably McLuhan would then ask what had led to such a differential interest in vision. To this the answer lies not in some antecedent visual encouragement, but in the total cognitive "set" that determines an interest in those objects or entities that happen to make themselves apparent through the medium of vision. Thus when an astronomer looks through his telescope he is not doing so because he has an artificially encouraged propensity for visual experience, but because he has an intellectual interest in those objects called stars. It so happens that the most obvious medium through which these entities make themselves apparent is light. Given the chance to negotiate with the heavenly bodies through some other medium, the astronomer would doubtless take advantage of it. And in fact nowadays he does. For certain stars emit radio waves in addition to light, and the radio-astronomer is perfectly willing to listen rather than look so long as the information that he gets thereby gives extra scientific substance to his cognitive notion of what a star really is.

In other words, cognitive interest determines the use to which the various human senses will be put, not vice versa; and this principle applies with equal force to the cultural evidence that McLuhan adduces in order to support his theory that the mind becomes biased by undue emphasis applied to one particular sense.

For example, to support his contention that illiterate Africans have a "low visual bias" he quotes a series of anecdotes about the misinterpretations of movies by an African audience. Actually, some of these stories are quite interesting, showing for instance that it requires a large measure of psychological training before an audience will accept the elementary cinematic conventions of tracking, panning, and close-up. Such evidence has no bearing upon so-called "visual bias." Instead it illustrates the well-known fact that before any significance can be attached to certain specimens of formal representation, the rules by which such representations make sense must be learned and understood.

The same objection applies to McLuhan's assertion that primitive tribesmen demonstrate their "low visual bias" by their failure to "see" the representation of space on a flat surface. Such a fact demonstrates no more than the subject's unfamiliarity with the grammar of two-dimensional space representation. One cannot conclude that there is an over-all limit upon the visual competence of a subject who fails in such a task, but only that his competence has not been trained to express itself in that particular way.

As it is there is a large body of evidence to show that within the area of their prescribed social interests, illiterate people exhibit a very high degree of visual competence. As Lévi-Strauss says in *The Savage Mind*, "Their extreme familiarity with their biological environment, the passionate attention which they pay to it and their precise knowledge of it has often struck enquirers as an indication of attitudes and preoccupations which distinguish natives from their white visitors."[1] And he quotes the observations made among the Tewa Indians of New Mexico by Robbins, Harrington, and Freire-

[1] Claude Lévi-Strauss, *The Savage Mind* (London: Weidenfeld, 1966), p. 5.

Marreco: "Small differences are noted . . . they have a name for every one of the coniferous trees of the region; in these cases differences are not conspicuous. The ordinary individual among the whites does not distinguish [them]. . . . Indeed, it would be possible to translate a treatise on botany into Tewa."[2]

Not, however, that one can assert from such evidence, in contradiction to McLuhan, that tribesmen have a *higher* over-all standard of visual competence than their civilized neighbors. That would be going from one extreme of absurdity to another.

The fact that members of a certain culture score badly when asked to perform a given cognitive task does not mean that their competence within the modality of the set task is comprehensively suspect. It means rather that their characteristic social preoccupations preclude any active cognitive interest in the tasks that *have* been set. The visual competence of a Walbiri tribesman, for instance, is demonstrated by the subtlety with which he discriminates between certain conventionally differentiated sand drawings. He is privy to the set of semantic options within which such signs acquire their meaning; and above all he is a member of a culture for which such acts of visual discrimination constitute an important qualification for significant membership.

Conversely it would be rash to conclude that a literate man (who, incidentally, "sees" the Muller-Lyer illusion when it is presented to him on paper) was visually incompetent simply because he failed to make allowances for refraction when spearing fish under water. The point

[2] W. W. Robbins, J. P. Harrington, and B. Freire-Marreco, "Ethnobiology of the Tewa Indians," Smithsonian Institution, Bureau of American Ethnology Bulletin No. 55 (Washington, D.C., 1916), pp. 9, 12.

is that very little trust can be placed in cross-cultural studies of cognitive competence; and any large-scale theory that relies on such methods is suspect.

The same goes, I think, for some of the conclusions drawn from the study of comparative literature, in spite of the fact that there are often striking differences in the relative emphasis given to visual detail. For example, Eric Auerbach has justifiably drawn attention to the strong visual emphasis in Homer and the relative absence of such imagery in the Old Testament. The story of how Ulysses acquired his scar in a hunting accident is filled with rich visual detail, while the tale of Abraham's sacrifice of Isaac is more or less free from such elaboration. Now although these differences are very dramatic, one would not be justified in concluding from them that the Greeks had a strong visual bias or that the Jews were particularly acoustic. All that one can say is that these two forms of *literature* are distinguished by this bias. Why are they distinguished in this manner? It is hard to say for certain, although it seems likely that the answer lies in the different social functions served respectively by each of the stories.

Thus the story of Abraham and Isaac does not survive in Hebrew scripture for the details of its surface narrative but, probably, for certain features whose *structural relationship* carry a social message concerning the legitimacy of Jewish descent. It is possible that visual detail is excluded for the simple reason that its presence might otherwise obscure the judicial message.

Not that I am insisting that this *is* the correct explanation, but simply that it is a plausible hypothesis, and one that ought to be considered before plunging into theories based upon dubious epistemology. And McLuhan makes the ensuing argument even harder to follow by at-

tributing the rising visual emphasis of Western civilization to the vicissitudes that language has undergone in
passing from speech to script, rather than to the discovery
and use of straightforward optical aids. That is to say,
he invites the reader to accept his suggestion that language should be regarded as an artificial aid to perception, on a par with all the mechanical extensions of the
special senses. Language, he argues, allows men to fix
and perpetuate their individual experiences in the form
of communicable fragments. A native communicant who
receives a set of such communiqués has his consciousness extended just as effectively as if he had looked at a
distant vista through a telescope. Language therefore is
a medium, and its effects upon the sensorium should
be considered in the same light.

This is seductive analogy, but serious difficulties arise
when it is pressed too far. Let me, however, postpone the
objections and develop McLuhan's argument on the assumption that we can think of language in this way.

To begin with, McLuhan emphasizes the obvious
fact that the natural form of human language is the
spoken one. As such it confers, by definition, an unusual
emphasis upon the faculty of hearing. Now since according to McLuhan any medium that stresses a single
sense in this way upsets the bias of the sensorium, one
might expect that undue dependence upon the spoken
word would exert dangerous strains in the manner specified. However, McLuhan insists that it does not violate
the *sensus communis* for the following reasons:

1. *Because of the synesthetic properties of sound itself.* McLuhan insists that "the ear world is hot and
hyperaesthetic," by which I take him to mean that any
message fortunate enough to be coded in terms of sound
carries an intrinsic bonus of collateral sensory experi-

ence. Speech therefore starts out with an initial exemption from the restrictions attendant upon stimuli arriving through all the other special senses.

2. *Because the subject matter of spoken speech is more fully representative of the total range of sensory experience than any other type of human communication.* According to this assertion, spoken language makes a wider range of concrete reference than, say, written language. The primitive speaker utters his thoughts more or less as they occur to him, thereby bodying forth the full content of his current experience. On such an assumption, if one were to collect an anthology of any given speaker's oral utterances, they would refer more comprehensively to the other senses than would a collection of written statements made by the same person.

3. *Because speech occurs in physical circumstances that call the other senses into play.* This is a much more reasonable suggestion than the previous two, since speech occurs within a context that is not monopolized by sound alone. That is to say, the significance of a given utterance is very incompletely characterized if the description is limited to a translation or a paraphrase of the utterance itself. There are many other parameters within which variations can be introduced in order to modulate the meaning of what is said or heard. The full significance of a given utterance is fully specified only when fixed values have been assigned to the following set of sensory variables:

Acoustic	a.	The lexical string itself. The naked message.
	b.	Its pitch, volume, timbre, stress, and rhythm.
Visual	a.	Facial expression of the speaker.
	b.	His manual gestures.

	c.	Visible distance between speakers and other participants.
	d.	Visual accessories to the scene that help to determine the significance of what is said, i.e., buildings, rostrums, pulpits, flags, bunting, masks.
Tactile	a.	Bodily contacts between speakers, i.e., prods, caresses, blows, and embraces.
	b.	Tactile sense of other people. Effects of crowding.
	c.	Physical temperature of the occasion.
Olfactory	a.	Smells of participating individuals. Use of incense, et cetera.

It is easy to take these complex accessories of speech for granted, and since so many of them vanish when language is committed to paper we are often unaware of the work we have to do before the full meanings can be eked out of a written statement. In fact, McLuhan argues that speech is relatively exempt from the sensory risks that attend all other artificial aids to perception, and his famous distinction between "hot" and "cool" media applies with special force to the acknowledged difference between written and spoken language.

McLuhan's term "hot," as I take it, is a slangy gloss upon the communications engineer's concept of semantic redundancy. This notion brings to our attention the fact that many messages carry more information than is strictly needed to get their implicit ideas across. English, for instance, is highly redundant; as one can tell from the fact that it is usually possible to eliminate a considerable number of words from a sentence and still compile an understandable telegram. The more words one eliminates, however, the more equivocal the meaning becomes, with the obvious result that the reader has to do more and more work inferring what is meant. In this sense spoken language is more redundant than the written form. Since semantic clues get lost in the act of transferring the message to paper, the reader is obliged to infer what was originally signified by filling in the gaps in accordance with rules derived from his previous experience. The term "hot," then, applies to those messages that have gaps in their information structure, requiring an act of positive inference from the recipient. This is a useful concept but, as we shall see later, McLuhan himself makes dubious and often unreliable use of it.

Having argued the cybernetic superiority of speech, McLuhan goes on to describe the particular dangers associated with the invention of writing. By his account, the discovery of the phonetic alphabet constituted a fatal lurch toward the overemployment of one isolated sense—vision. For language would now be transcribed into a form that excluded the multiple sensory overtones associated with the spoken word. That is to say, it would work independently of

1. The synesthetic overtones of sound itself.
2. The orchestration of all the other sensations that attend the delivery of speech.
3. The improvisational variety of direct speech.

In addition, however, to the sensory impoverishment associated with such *negative* features of written language, McLuhan claims to have identified certain *positive* blemishes inherent in the substance of visible text.

According to McLuhan a fatal psychological decorum descends upon the scribe, with the immediate result that his thought is laid out in long lines of disciplined symbols. In place of the hesitant creativity of speech, we meet the dull regimentation of written language. Script thus encourages a formal sense of strict logical entailment that imposes, to repeat McLuhan's words, a "spurious intelligibility" upon our experience of the world. The innocent victim of literacy therefore falls prey to a stultified form of thought and loses the capacity to conceive the world in a rounded plenary style. Not only that. In learning to scan the orderly lines of text the reader unwittingly assumes a single point of view, thereby conferring upon himself an unnatural bias in favor of three-dimensional perspective.

Suffering all these effects together, the skilled reader becomes a sort of psychological cripple, confined to the wheel chair of logical thought, incapable of venturing over the rough ground of intuition and imagination. In *The Gutenberg Galaxy* McLuhan quotes Yeats:

> Locke sank into a swoon
> The garden died
> God took the spinning jenny
> Out of his side.

and comments:

> The Lockean swoon was the hypnotic trance induced by stepping up the visual component in experience until it filled the field of attention. Psychologists define hypnosis as the filling of the field of attention by one sense only. At such a moment "the garden" dies. That is, the garden indicates the interplay of all the senses in haptic harmony. With the instressed concern with one sense only, the mechanical principle of abstraction and repetition emerges into explicit form. Technology is explicitness,

as Lyman Bryson said. And explicitness means the spelling out of one thing at a time, one sense at a time, one mental or physical operation at a time.[3]

Since so much is balanced upon this statement it is unfortunate that McLuhan should have misdescribed hypnosis in such a careless way. For the fact is that hypnosis cannot be defined in the fashion McLuhan suggests. If it was, biologists would go into a trance every time they looked down their microscopes and blind men would become suggestible immediately they began to run their hands over a page of Braille. For each of these episodes involves the filling of the field of attention by one sense at the expense of the others. Indeed, as I have already indicated, that is what we mean by paying attention. Hypnosis is something very different altogether. The monopoly of the subject's attention may be a necessary condition for hypnosis, but it is by no means a sufficient one. It is the peculiar *quality* of the field that induces the trance—a calculated monotony accompanied by certain insistent suggestions. By no stretch of the imagination can such a phenomenon be likened to what happens when someone becomes accustomed to print.

This apart, most of the characteristic errors in McLuhan's seductive hypothesis arise from the fact that he has slipped past our guard with the spurious assumption that one can consider language as a technical medium that exists independently of the mind that uses it. In this way it becomes easy to compare it with any of the other physical artifacts through which the range of perception is increased. Such an opinion, however, embodies a category mistake; for language is not just an optional appendage of the human mind, but a constituent feature

[3] *The Gutenberg Galaxy*, pp. 17–18.

of its ongoing activity. Language in fact bears the same relationship to the concept of mind that legislation bears to the concept of parliament: it is a competence forever bodying itself in a series of concrete performances.

Seeing language in this way, as a relationship between competence and performance, one can begin to appreciate that the substance through which language is expressed is a matter of relative indifference. Let me amplify this point a little. The English neurologist Hughlings Jackson realized more than a hundred years ago that language is simply the expression of an underlying capacity to make propositions. In order to utter or "outer" such mental assertions, the subject has at his disposal a wide variety of discriminable substances—visual, acoustic, and even tactile—any one of which can be organized into patterns of communicable assertion. But as the linguist Ferdinand de Saussure recognized, linguistic signs bear an arbitrary, though consistent, relationship to the concepts they signify. All that is required of them is that they consistently stand for what they do and that they not be confused with any similar sign that stands for something different. In other words, the structure of language is determined not by the material from which it is made but by the internal relationships that prevail among its component parts. It is characterized, therefore, by the generative rules that constitute its ongoing practices, not by the physical peculiarities of the matter that passes between speaker and listener (or between writer and reader).

De Saussure illustrates this important distinction with reference to the game of chess. The pieces can be made of any material one chooses. The pawns and bishops, kings and rooks can be fashioned in any style that catches the manufacturer's fancy and the board can be no larger than a pocket handkerchief or as big as a cricket pitch. All these variables are irrelevant to the conduct of chess itself, which is characterized by the rules in accordance with which certain strategies are initiated. The game can be played by two people facing each other over the same board, but nothing is lost when the contest is conducted over the telephone, using pieces of paper to record the successive moves. The moves are made, and their significance is understood, with reference to a set of constitutive rules that are systematized in such a way that any tactical novelty can be accommodated so long as it is embodied in accordance with the given constitution.

This concept of language as a set of generative rules has been recently developed by linguists such as Noam Chomsky, who maintain, moreover, that in addition to the acknowledged constraints upon the structure of linguistic behavior, there is an underlying system of universal rules in accordance with which the surface regulations of all conventional grammars are selected in the first place. In *Language and Mind*, Chomsky writes:

The principles that determine the form of grammar and that select a grammar of the appropriate form on the basis of certain data constitute a subject that might, following a traditional usage, be termed "universal grammar." The study of universal grammar, so understood, is a study of the nature of human intellectual capacities. It tries to formulate the necessary and sufficient conditions that a system must meet to qualify as a potential human language, conditions that are not accidentally true of the existing human languages, but that are rather rooted in the human "language capacity," and thus constitute the innate organization that determines what counts as linguistic experience and what knowledge of language arises on the basis of this experience. Universal grammar, then, constitutes an explanatory theory of a much deeper sort than particular grammar, although the particular grammar of a language can also be regarded as an explanatory theory.[4]

The reader will immediately recognize that this assertion more or less contradicts the linguistic relativity that McLuhan extracted and exploited from Whorf. Without wishing to disparage Whorf's achievement in the area of anthropological linguistics, I would suggest that Chomsky's notion of deep universal grammar may actually include and explain the various differences noted by Whorf. If this turns out to be the case, we would be forced to account for the special peculiarities of the Hopi world picture with reference to psychological principles that lie outside the study of communications as such.

This is not the place to debate the Whorf-Chomsky controversy in more detail. It is sufficient to say that McLuhan seems unaware that the controversy exists; and that any theory of human communication that does not take its implied differences into consideration has very little right to be taken seriously.

In addition to the difficulties that arise when language is regarded as a medium rather than as a dynamic relationship between competence and performance, there are many factual flaws in McLuhan's famous proposal.

1. *In connection with assertions about the sensory richness of speech.* To begin with, there is no reliable evidence to support his claim that the sense of hearing is hotter or more redundant than any of the other sense modalities. The well-known phenomenon of synesthesia,

[4] Noam Chomsky, *Language and Mind* (New York: Harcourt, Brace, 1968), p. 24.

whereby a stimulus applied in one sensory department excites sensation in the others, is not peculiar to hearing. It is true, of course, that a note struck on the piano will often excite collateral sensations of color and that a deep acoustic tone will sometimes excite a feeling of tactile "presence." But these effects work reciprocally as well. Subjects will frequently report that certain colors are associated in their minds with fixed acoustic pitches and so on.

Secondly, while the delivery of the spoken word is certainly faster and more direct than anything written down, one cannot conclude that the range of its sensory reference is thereby wider and more comprehensive. Certain specimens of written language may be loaded with rich sensory references, while spoken utterances may be confined to relatively abstract announcements. To say this is not to deny that various channels of communication tend to impose characteristic features upon the messages that are passing through them. Written prose is undoubtedly more formal in general than ordinary speech. But on the other hand there are enormous differences within the oral mode. The grammar of a political address is far more conventional than that of a political argument, and telephone conversations sound quite different from a chat over the garden wall. These, however, are well-acknowledged distinctions and have no bearing whatsoever upon sensory emphasis as McLuhan understands the term.

Moreover there is no evidence to show that literacy has usurped the advantages to be gained from the sensory context within which speech occurs. People continue to face each other when they talk. They still avail themselves of subtle clues derived from facial expression and manual gesture. In fact it could be argued that the sensitivity to such accessory variations has increased in literate communities, and that civilized men take much closer note of the fleeting nuances of facial expression than savages do. Certainly it is true to say that literature has created an unprecedented interest in the minute variables of individual temperament, with the result that a public that has been exposed to such a training is likely to pay very close attention to the physiognomic clues that bear witness to such variety. I am not saying that this is necessarily true, but it is at least a plausible hypothesis, and one that any investigator of the subject would do well to acknowledge even if he were in a position to refute it later.

By the same token it seems unlikely that literacy would, by its very nature, have impoverished the richness of spoken language. Quite the reverse. The expressive possibilities offered by being able to write thoughts down after mature consideration would seem, on first principles at least, to be a friendly condition for linguistic innovation. In fact the advent of literacy, far from extinguishing the imagination, has vastly increased the number of its expressive options. Indeed, it is hard to overestimate the subtle reflexive effects of literacy upon the creative imagination, providing as it does a cumulative deposit of ideas, images, and idioms upon whose rich and appreciating funds every artist enjoys an unlimited right of withdrawal.

2. *In connection with McLuhan's assertions about the peculiarly visual properties of print.* McLuhan asserts that there is an exclusive linearity about script, so that the rich manifold of subjective experience becomes distorted by having to be issued in the form of a symbolic strip. Speech, by contrast, has a plural simultaneity that allows human thought to be deployed in a much more

commodious form. Even on first principles this suggestion seems wrong. Speech is just as linear as script—more so in fact. Only one sound, after all, can be issued at a time, with the result that an oral utterance can only pay itself out in the form of a long string. This is vividly—and (to McLuhan) very damagingly—brought out by the fact that it is possible to reproduce human speech on a narrow ribbon of magnetized tape. How linear can one get?

To be fair, there *is* a sense in which it is true to assert that speech is "simultaneous." In order to understand the meaning of a sentence it is necessary for the listener to hold in his memory at least a temporary record of all the words that have just been uttered, so that each *new* word can then take its place in a context that gives it significance. If the sounds were erased concurrently with the development of the speech, we would hear only one word at a time and no meaning would accumulate. In this sense a speech must be grasped in its simultaneous entirety, otherwise it would fail in its function *as a speech*.

But the same holds true for written sentences. If we simply read one word at a time, and erased the traces of all preceding script, the written display would enter our minds in unrelated fragments and never accumulate its assigned implication. Insofar as there is any difference between the "simultaneity" of speech and that of script, the bias is somewhat in favor of script. Reading experiments have shown that the eye does not advance along the written line in smooth succession; nor does it move forward in small equal jerks. Instead it seems to "take in" large irregular chunks of text, whose boundaries are determined more by the various quanta of meaning they contain than by any visible breaks in the contours of the display itself.

Not only that. The reader tends to flick his eyes all over the page, backward from the central reading point to remind himself of what has gone before, forward in an effort to confirm premature guesses about the meaning of half-read sentences. Taking all these effects together, the page assembles itself before the reader's eye not as a linear string of visible symbols but as a panorama of overlapping "instantanees."

McLuhan claims that script (and a fortiori print) influences the reader as a visual medium, overemploying his eye at the expense of the ear. This assertion depends upon a willful confusion between visibility and legibility. For the visibility of script is only a necessary condition of our being able to read it. Sufficient conditions for legibility are provided by the fact that the various symbols it comprises are clearly distinguishable from one another—a condition, incidentally, that is also satisfied by Braille. In fact, it is characteristic of reading that the better we are at it, the more unconscious we become of having to use our eyes. We only "see" the written page when it bears a foreign text, or when slipshod handwriting makes it hard to distinguish the various letters. The accomplished native reader, confronted by a clear page of script in his own tongue, "gets" the meaning without "seeing" the display that embodies it. This, in fact, is part of the definition of reading.

McLuhan would probably file a counterclaim to this objection to the effect that, in the process of becoming so familiar with written symbols that they effectively disappear, the eye had become concurrently overactive; and that even if the accomplished reader no longer "sees" the text that he reads, his sensorium has nevertheless been irreversibly biased in favor of vision in the process. There is, however, no example to show that children become more visually accomplished with the achievement of literacy.

McLuhan claims incidentally that although manuscript has many important features in common with print, it is nonetheless only halfway toward the glaring visibility of type. According to him handwriting preserves a saving remnant of the original audio-tactility of speech. Taking his cue from the work of Henry Chaytor, he insists that the mediaeval reader mumbled the text out loud and that silent reading only became the fashion when the improved legibility of print eliminated such a necessity.

There are several weak points in this argument too. To start with, there is no consistent evidence to show that reading out loud was associated exclusively with manuscript—the occasional anecdotes frequently quoted on this subject are not enough to base a theory on. And even if it were true, there is little to indicate that the murmuring scholar was thereby investing the visual text with the warm tones of spoken language. As for the so-called tactility of manuscript, it is little more than a figure of speech anyway, and whatever substance it does have depends on the visual features of the script.

Even if it were true that print overdeveloped the visual sense, it would be false to conclude that the subject thereby falls prey to three-dimensional interpretations of space. There are no intrinsic three-dimensional clues provided by sight. Spatial significance is only conferred upon the retinal information through the collateral experience provided by the other senses; and even then it is only

acquired as a hard-won cognitive construct whose constitutive features comprise a set of rules. In obedience to
these rules, the subject learns to apply "spatial" significance to such clues as convergent sight lines, texture
gradients, overlapping contours, and so on. These clues
stand for nothing in their own right; they await a cognitive equation to relate them all in the manner prescribed.

As for the suggestion that central perspective arose as
a result of print, it seems rather surprising that the work
of Masaccio should have anticipated that of Gutenberg.
It is true, of course, that perspective drawing only began
to predominate after the sixteenth century, but there is
no evidence to show that the development of print was
responsible. The whole point about inventions of this
sort is that they have an intrinsic momentum of their
own. Once discovered they tend to monopolize the
pictorial imagination and eventually become the pre-
vailing mode.

The same principle holds for the discovery of oil painting. When Van Eyck found that thin glazes of oil allowed him to depict surface detail with an unprecedented
accuracy, he thereby opened up new vistas of pictorial
possibility that other painters hurried to exploit not, as
McLuhan would have it, through some obscure encouragement offered by print, but because of the implicit
creative excitement of the thing itself. If there is any
point in asking why such developments took hold, the
question should take the form of inquiring why print,
perspective, and oil painting *all* emerged within the same
century. Few art historians would be prepared to give a
definitive answer. It is in fact notoriously hard to account for changes in aesthetic style, and no advantage is
to be gained from simplifying the issue by attributing

the developments to unique incidents in the history of technology.

We come now to McLuhan's assertion that the peculiar idiom of atomic determinism was inextricably associated with the segmented linearity of alphabetic script. To support this claim McLuhan emphasizes the well-established fact that the Chinese, who wrote in ideograms, gave no place to atomic entities and organized their characteristic world picture in accordance with principles that closely resemble those of modern field theory. But a well-accredited expert on the subject is reluctant to assume that this is more than a coincidence:

It is a striking, and perhaps significant, fact that the languages of all those civilisations which developed atomic theories were alphabetic. Just as an almost infinite variety of words may be formed by different combinations of the relatively small number of letters in an alphabet, so the idea was natural enough that a large number of bodies with different properties might be composed by the association in different ways of a very small number of constituent elementary particles. . . . On the other hand, the Chinese written character is an organic whole, a Gestalt, and minds accustomed to an ideographic language would perhaps hardly have been so open to the idea of an atomic constitution of matter. Nevertheless, the argument is weakened by the fact that the 214 radicals into which the Chinese lexicographers eventually reduced what they considered the fundamental elements of the written characters were essentially atomic, and an immense variety of words ("molecules") were formed by their combinations. Moreover, the combinations of the components of the Symbolic Correlation groups of five were understood from very early times to produce all natural phenomena . . . while there is a certain plausibility in the correlation between alphabetism and atomism, the argument cannot be pressed too strongly.[5]

Insofar as Needham is prepared to hazard a guess as to the forces responsible for such differences in world picture, he favors, in contrast to McLuhan, a somewhat more sociological interpretation: "Can we consider it a mere coincidence that [Taoist organicism] arose in a highly organized society where conservancy-dictated bureaucratism was dominant, while [Democritean-Epicurean atomism] arose in a world of city-states and individual merchant-adventurers? I believe that we cannot."[6]

On a somewhat different tack McLuhan also suggests that the techniques of formal logic could never have emerged without the discovery of alphabetic writing. In this he is backed up by more recent authority. In "The Consequences of Literacy," published in 1968, Jack Goody and Ian Watt wrote:

> The kinds of analysis involved in the syllogism, and in the other forms of logical procedure, are clearly dependent upon writing, indeed upon a form of writing sufficiently simple and cursive to make possible widespread and habitual recourse both to the recording of verbal statements and then to the dissecting of them. It is probable that it is only the analytic process that writing itself entails, the written formalization of sounds and syntax, which make possible the habitual separating out into formally distinct units of the various cultural elements whose

[5] Joseph Needham, *Science and Civilization in China* (New York and London: Cambridge University Press, 1954), IV, Sec. 1, 13–14.
[6] *Ibid.*, II, 338.

indivisible wholeness is the essential basis of the "mystical participation" which Lévy-Bruhl regards as characteristic of the thinking of non-literate peoples.[7]

Nevertheless, as Goody himself goes on to say, "neither Lévy-Bruhl nor any other advocate of a radical dichotomy between primitive and civilised thought [has] been able to account for the considerable persistence of non-logical thought in modern literate societies." If, as McLuhan suggests, the experience of print overwhelms the power of metaphoric thought, it seems rather odd that Newton—who was, by McLuhan's account, the arch victim (and villain) of the Gutenberg tyranny— should have spent at least half his intellectual effort in constructing a magical system that even now proves a serious embarrassment to historians who would like to appropriate him to the pure scientific tradition. Rather it would seem that print, as a medium, gave Newton's genius room to maneuver in both idioms.

The fact is that the forces at work in determining the preferred modes of human thought are far more plural and obscure than McLuhan would allow. Doubtless the various media *have* had their characteristic effects, but in acknowledging such influences there is no need to emphasize them to the exclusion of everything else—especially not with reference to an epistemological theory that has no foundation in neuropsychological reality.

As a summary, I prefer the more modest proposal advanced by Kathleen Gough:

Literacy appears to be, above all, an *enabling* factor, permitting large-scale organization, the critical accumulation, storage and retrieval of knowledge,

[7] In Jack Goody, ed., *Literacy in Traditional Societies* (London and New York: Cambridge University Press, 1968, 1969), p. 68.

the systematic use of logic, the pursuit of science and the elaboration of the arts. Whether, or with what emphases, these developments will occur seems to depend less on the intrinsic knowledge of writing than on the overall development of the society's technology and social structure, and perhaps, also, on the character of its relations with other societies. *If* they occur, however, there seems little doubt of Goody and Watt's contention that the use of writing as a dominant communications medium will impose certain broad forms on their emergence, of which syllogistic reasoning and linear codifications of reality may be examples. The partial supersession of writing by new communications media will no doubt throw into relief more and more of the specific implications of literacy.[8]

Which brings us in conclusion to television, the correct analysis of which might, as Kathleen Gough implies, throw the effects of literacy into sharp and informative relief. Unfortunately McLuhan fails to take any disciplined advantage of this opportunity: his descriptions of television are vitiated by the same eccentricities that infect his speculations about typography.

To start with, he makes a groundless assertion about the inherent qualities of the medium to the effect that they go some way toward reversing the damage inflicted by the structural peculiarities of print. According to him television is not really a visual medium at all, but an audio-tactile one, which restores to the viewer some of the haptic richness associated with manuscript. How does he arrive at these bizarre conclusions?

The auditory aspect is quite straightforward. The image is accompanied by sound. No argument. What about

[8] *Ibid.*, p. 84.

the tactility then? "The TV image is not a *still* shot. It is not photo in any sense, but a ceaselessly forming contour of things limned by the scanning-finger. The resulting plastic contour appears by light *through*, not light *on*, and the image so formed has the quality of sculpture and icon, rather than of picture."[9]

Once again we have a vivid example of a metaphor illicitly conjured into a concrete reality. For although the television picture *is* assembled by a rapidly scanning electronic beam, there is only a metaphorical similarity between this mechanism and the behavior of a finger following a tactile contour. For the process takes place so fast that the spectator couldn't possibly know that it had happened. Even if the "scan" were slow enough for the spectator to appreciate it, the experience itself would still be visual. As for the distinction between "light on" and "light through," the source of the beam that carries the information has nothing to do with the picture as seen by the viewer. A movie projected from behind the screen looks exactly the same as one projected from the front. Television is simply another form of rear projection, and the fact that it is makes no difference to the quality of the viewer's experience.

McLuhan's next assertion is even more nonsensical. The television image, he says, is poorly defined. Compared to the images on a movie screen those on television invariably seem murky and blurred. No one could deny this. But far from seeing it as a drawback, McLuhan conceives it as the essential psychological advantage offered by television. Because the image is low in information, it is relatively "cold," demanding active inference by the viewer before its full meaning can be appreciated. Through having his intellectual activity thus recruited,

[9] *Understanding Media*, p. 313.

the viewer is, by McLuhan's account, deeply involved in the picture, which he helps to build. Like the mediaeval scholar who eked out the meaning of his illegible manuscript by reading it out loud, the modern viewer ekes out the meaning of the blurred images upon his screen, and thereby invests them with a peculiar vitality.

This is an absurd suggestion and it deserves to be destroyed forthwith. The type of psychological transaction that takes place while "filling in" the information gaps contained in a poor image has no bearing upon the sense of conscious involvement. The picture gets "completed" in accordance with purely automatic rules of visual inference; and if this activity ever reaches consciousness, it does so not in the form of participant pleasure, but as a subliminal exhaustion that actually undermines attention. There is in fact an *inverse* relationship between the quality of the picture and the degree of conscious psychological involvement. The poorer the image the more alienated the viewer becomes from it. He starts to adjust the brightness controls and finally switches stations in disgust.

What I think McLuhan has done is to confuse the low information content of television with the artful simplification of sketches and cartoons. The pattern of a drawing is carefully conceived on the understanding that certain key lines will stand for all those that have been omitted. The picture so formed is strategically simplified in order to achieve a certain pictorial effect. In contrast, the television picture is haphazardly incomplete, so that the viewer has no formal clues to guide his psychological participation.

The same holds true for the conventions of painting. When Corot blurred the foliage of his trees he did so in order to represent its slight movement. The blurring of television represents nothing, but is instead an adventitious nuisance interposed between the viewer and the picture he is meant to receive. What is remarkable about television is the fact that such a large audience *tolerates* its inadequacy. In order to explain this, one must resort to social explanations rather than to dubious derivatives of Gestalt psychology. People tolerate the poor image of television not because they get so much pleasure out of filling in its gaps, but because it is relatively cheap, enormously convenient, and because its messages fill certain long-felt wants (which, incidentally, the various commercial companies do everything to exploit and shape to their own advantage).

Apart from these dubious interpretations of the quality of the medium itself, McLuhan rightly draws our attention to the effects of the presence of television in every home. Just as the telegraph and the railroad brought people of the world closer together—with all the diverse and equivocal effects that such propinquity breeds—so television introduces the inhabitants of one nation to those of another, thereby establishing a certain measure of common experience.

As usual, however, McLuhan exaggerates and distorts the details of this fickle communion. According to him the electronic network has re-tribalized modern man, overcome the fissiparous influence of print, and restored the human race to its rightful place in the "global village."

A stirring slogan, but is it anything more? The so-called community called into existence by television has very little more than a metaphorical affinity with a village, whose distinctive character is significantly defined by the face-to-face collaboration of the people who form its enduring nucleus. A genuine village community exists only through the local institutions that embody the shared interests of its inhabitants. Such institutions more or less effectively exclude the participation of outsiders who do not contribute directly to their upkeep.

It is true, of course, that television allows us to share the experiences of those who live at a great distance. But the whole point about such "shared" experiences is that they are essentially vicarious, and have little or nothing in common with the experiences that define the characteristic collectivism of village life. For example, when Americans viewed the television pictures of the Vietnam war—especially the live transmissions—their concern and interest were expressed mainly for the condition of "our boys out there." That is to say, television illustrated the fate of *American* "villagers." Insofar as television excited concern on behalf of the *Vietnamese*, it did not do so because the viewers recognized them as fellow villagers, but rather because they acknowledged them as human personalities to whom certain generalized obligations were due.

In fact, it is characteristic of the outcries such programs produced that appeal to *general principle* formed an essential part of their rhetoric. Not that this is a bad thing, but it is important to distinguish such abstract principles from the concrete scruples that control the way in which tribal villagers behave toward one another. For the essential feature of tribal or village morality is that it is *not* realized with reference to general principles—or at least not to principles that can be articulated independently of the contexts to which they immediately apply. The moral imperatives that shape the collective conduct of village life are inseparable from the immediate circumstances which they control. They are embedded in the social context that gives them meaning, and it is very doubtful whether the people who behave in accordance with them would ever recognize their existence as an independent body of moral regulations.

What is more, the principles with reference to which American liberals both initiated and justified their concern were created by the very traditions of literacy that McLuhan suspects. Without such a printed menu of acknowledged human rights it is unlikely that the television experience of distant atrocity would have provoked anything more than a voyeur's interest. In other words, any "village" sentiment that television creates is almost entirely parasitic upon the printed arguments that gave them priority in the first place.

McLuhan has also underestimated the destructive features of television, and he has overlooked those which actually undermine the sense of global community.

For a start, there are now so many documentary and current-affairs programs that insofar as television *has* enlarged the family of man, it has done so beyond the point where genuine sentiment can be expressed for all its constituent members. There is after all a limit upon the number of moral obligations that any individual can feel himself capable of discharging. Confronted as he is now by the image of so many human predicaments, the spectator becomes confused, frustrated, and finally, in self-protection, isolationist. He almost deliberately exempts himself from the concern that these programs would otherwise seem to solicit.

This sense of alienation is reinforced by certain sensory features of the medium contrary to what McLuhan asserts. Television is strikingly visual and the images it presents are curiously dissociated from all the other senses. The viewer sits watching them all in the drab comfort of his own home, cut off from the pain, heat, and smell of what is actually going on. Even the sound is artificial. (McLuhan ignores the fact that many news-reels are accompanied by the commentator's "voice over" and not by the natural din of the scene itself.) All these effects serve to distance the viewer from the scenes he is watching, and eventually he falls into the uncon-scious belief that the events that happen on television are going on in some unbelievably remote theater of hu-man activity.

The alienating effect is magnified by the fact that the television screen reduces all images to the same visual quality. Atrocity and entertainment alternate with one another on the same rectangle of bulging glass. Comedy and politics merge into one continuous ribbon of trans-mission. It is hard to see how ordinary village life can survive under such conditions, let alone that of a global village.

McLuhan has more or less overlooked these considera-tions, distracted as he is by the idea that modern elec-tronics has externalized the nervous system of man. According to him, the vast network of electrical commu-nications that now links the distant corners of the earth has created a collective cosmic analogue of the individual brain. Instead of cogitating in the solitude they once created for themselves under the influence of print, men can now think together through the permissive medium of a synthetic nervous system that surrounds the globe. This of course is an exciting and vivid metaphor, and it certainly serves to emphasize the ease with which distant people can come into some sort of contact with one another. Taken too literally it obscures all those conditions that determine the *breaches* in human cooperation.

McLuhan's notion of the global nervous system and the almost identical idea of the noosphere as formulated by Teilhard de Chardin have a strange poetic affinity. Thus Teilhard in *The Phenomenon of Man*:

> The recognition and isolation of a new era in evolution, the era of noogenesis, obliges us to distinguish correlatively a support proportionate to the operation—that is to say, yet another membrane in the majestic assembly of telluric layers. A glow ripples outward from the first spark of conscious reflection. The point of ignition grows larger. The fire spreads in ever widening circles till finally the whole planet is covered with incandescence. Only one interpretation, only one name can be found worthy of this grand phenomenon. Much more coherent and just as extensive as any preceding layer, it is really a new layer, the "thinking layer", which, since its germination at the end of the Tertiary period, has spread over and above the world of planets and animals. In other words, outside and above the biosphere there is the noosphere.[10]

Apart from the social reality that Teilhard's noosphere and McLuhan's global nervous system somewhat incoherently embody, it is important to realize the strong element of wish fulfillment they express. Both men, as I have already indicated, are Catholics and as such give enormous and understandable priority to the fundamental spiritual unity of man. Any institution, natural or artificial, which gives *secular* thought world-wide expres-

[10] Pierre Teilhard de Chardin, *The Phenomenon of Man* (London: Collins, 1959), p. 182.

sion would seem, on first principles at least, to be a congenial circumstance within which to establish a consensus of *piety* too.

Catholics who once looked to the Roman church as an institution that might have realized such aspirations were obviously disappointed by the events that followed the Reformation. But while men like Chesterton retreated into the dubious consolations of nostalgia, McLuhan mounted a much more adventurous crusade on behalf of the lost consensus, seeking aids to its recovery in the very culture that usurped it. This paradoxical enterprise relies upon the optimistic identification of certain unexpectedly hopeful features in the structure of an otherwise corrupt regime. In other words, while deploring the secular individualism supposedly characteristic of societies based upon print, he claimed to have recognized certain technical developments—such as television and radio—that could, if exploited intelligently, do much to reverse the profane tendencies of the society that had invented such devices.

The devil defeated by his own ingenuity! Notice the cyclical justice enacted by such a process. It cannot be an accident that McLuhan, through the medium of Joyce, laid such friendly emphasis upon the work of Giovanni Battista Vico, a historian who also liked to imagine that human destiny revolved through circles of regenerative repetition. Certainly some of the criticisms leveled at Vico apply with peculiar force to McLuhan too.[11]

[11] "Vico," wrote Benedetto Croce, "was in a state similar to that of drunkenness; confusing categories with facts, he felt absolutely certain a priori of what the facts would say; instead of letting them speak for themselves he put his own words into their mouth. A common illusion with him was to seem to see connexions between things where there was really none. This made him turn every hypothetical

The point is that when history is conceived on a gigantic scale it is almost impossible not to misuse facts and quotations in the way that both Vico and McLuhan do. The tide of human events becomes so vast that, as McLuhan himself suggests, conventional intellectual etiquette seems irrelevant and tangential. The sheer size of the panorama reduces all formal argument to triviality. On such a broad background, even factual details lose their concrete individuality and, like iridescent oil patches on the surface of a wet road, stretch, swim, and glimmer with vague equivocal significance.

Impressed as he obviously is by this Heraclitean flux, McLuhan, like Vico, adapted his whole literary style to fit it. Linear exposition is abandoned in favor of what he calls the "mosaic approach"; and by means of techniques that are closely copied from those of the Dada movement he assembles a collage of slogans, facts, and quotations through whose artful juxtaposition he hopes to reproduce the simultaneous present of historical reality, as did Joyce in *Finnegans Wake*: "riverrun, past Eve and Adam's, from swerve of shore to bend of bay, brings us by a commodius vicus of recirculation back to Howth Castle and Environs."

Unfortunately this stream of historical consciousness offers no fixed point from which the reader can take his

---

conjunction into a certainty, and read in other writers instead of their actual words things that they had never written, but which were internally spoken by himself unawares and projected into the writings of others. Exactitude was for him an impossibility, and in his mental excitement and exaltation he almost despised it. . . . Fanciful etymologies, daring and groundless mythological interpretations, changes of name and date, exaggerations of fact, false quotations are met with throughout his pages." (Benedetto Croce, *Giambattista Vico*, trans. R. G. Collingwood [London: Latimer, 1913], p. 152).

critical bearings. Before he has time to object to any single fact or assertion it has changed its shape on the surface of the current or swept out of view altogether. Anyone who complains is simply dismissed as a victim of the Gutenberg tyranny.

By writing in this way McLuhan has also cunningly appropriated all the standards of criticism and protected himself from the very possibility of rebuttal. He has, according to his disciples, redefined the entire notion of inquiry and in doing so has established exclusive rights for choosing the principles by which any criticism of his own thesis might be made.

Far from being overawed by this critical impermeability, McLuhan's opponents regard it as the characteristic flaw in the whole enterprise. For theories deserve attention in direct proportion to their capacity to withstand judgment in accordance with independent standards. A descriptive hypothesis that can only survive by disqualifying even the relevance of valid counterassertions is little short of myth.

Not that McLuhan would be in the least dismayed by having his work described in this way, for he believes that "in myth this fusion and telescoping of phases of process becomes a kind of explanation or mode of intelligibility." This assertion leaves no room for distinguishing between competing myths. One is as good as any other. The whole point about genuine explanations is that they must have a certain degree of acknowledged brittleness. That is to say, any proposition that purports to explain something must, in order to qualify as an explanation, remain open to contradiction. Otherwise it becomes impossible to choose between competing assertions, and the whole notion of understanding gives way to caprice.

In spite of all these objections one is left with the disturbing suspicion that McLuhan is "on to something." Not with respect to any of his grand theories, most of which are too generalized and incoherent to be of much value—nor indeed on account of any of his specific insights, few of which bear close scrutiny—but because he has successfully convened a debate on a subject that has been neglected too long. For all the maddening slogans, paradoxes, and puns; for all the gross breaches of intellectual etiquette—or perhaps even because of them all— McLuhan has forced us to attend to the various media through which we gain our knowledge of the world. On the basis of *The Mechanical Bride* alone he deserves an important place in the history of cultural criticism; and he will always be remembered for the part he played in launching the magazine *Exploration*, through whose pages many critics first became aware of the fact that they had never before intelligently used their physical senses. The medium may not be the message exactly, but it certainly imposes subtle constraints that we are constantly apt to overlook. Staring at the view beyond the window we have become unconscious of the fact that glass, for all its transparency, confers optical peculiarities upon the various scenes at which we like to think we are gazing directly.

I can still recall the intense excitement with which I first read McLuhan in 1960. Not that I remember a single observation that I now hold to be true, nor indeed a single theory that even begins to hold water. And yet, as a result of reading him, I first began to look at print as a thing in itself; I became aware of the peculiar idioms associated with using the telephone; I began to see photographs not just as pictures of the world around but as peculiar objects existing in their own right, often usurping the reality that they supposedly represented. The special idioms associated with radio became glaringly apparent; and as someone who has subsequently spent much time trying to devise and shape programs for television I am grateful for the way in which McLuhan alerted me to the odd properties of the medium itself. And yet I can rehabilitate no actual truth from what I read. Perhaps McLuhan has accomplished the greatest paradox of all, creating the possibility of truth by shocking us all with a gigantic system of lies.

> The special rhetorical purpose . . . is to overcome the mental inertia of human beings, which mental inertia is constantly landing them in the strange predicament of both seeing a thing and not seeing it. When people's perceptions are in this condition, they must, in the strictest sense of the words, be made to renew their acquaintance with things. They must be made to see them anew, as if for the first time.[12]

[12] Hugh Kenner, *Paradox in Chesterton* (New York: Sheed & Ward, 1947), p. 43.

SHORT BIBLIOGRAPHY

Selected Books and Articles by McLuhan

BOOKS

The Mechanical Bride: Folklore of Industrial Man. New York: Vanguard, 1951.

Selected Poetry of Tennyson. New York: Rinehart, 1956.

Explorations in Communication, with E. S. Carpenter. Boston: Beacon Press, 1960.

The Gutenberg Galaxy: The Making of Typographic Man. Toronto: University of Toronto Press, 1962.

Understanding Media: The Extensions of Man. New York: McGraw-Hill, 1964.

Voices of Literature, edited with Richard J. Shoeck. Two vols. New York: Holt, 1965, 1966.

The Medium Is the Massage: An Inventory of Effects, with Quentin Fiore. New York: Random House, 1967.

Counterblast, with Harley Parker. New York: Harcourt, Brace, 1969.

Through the Vanishing Point: Space in Poetry and Painting, with Harley Parker. New York: Harper & Row, 1968.

War and Peace in the Global Village, with Quentin Fiore. New York: McGraw-Hill, 1968.
From Cliché to Archetype. New York: Viking, 1970.

ARTICLES

"G. K. Chesterton: A Practical Mystic." *Dalhousie Review*, Vol. 15, 1936.
"Edgar Poe's Tradition." *Sewanee Review*, Vol. 52, No. 1, January 1944.
"Wyndham Lewis: Lemuel in Lilliput." *St. Louis University Studies in Honor of St. Thomas Aquinas*. Vol. 2, 1944.
"Poetic vs. Rhetorical Exegesis." *Sewanee Review*, Vol. 52, No. 2, April 1944.
"The Analogical Mirrors." In Kenyon Review Critics, *Gerard Manley Hopkins*. New York: New Directions, 1946.
"An Ancient Quarrel in Modern America." *The Classical Journal*, Vol. 41, No. 4, January 1946.
"Footprints in the Sands of Crime." *Sewanee Review*, Vol. 54, No. 4, Autumn 1946.
Introduction to Hugh Kenner, *Paradox in Chesterton*. London: Sheed & Ward, 1948.
"The Southern Quality." *Sewanee Review*, Vol. 55, No. 1, July 1947.
"Tennyson and Picturesque Poetry." *Essays in Criticism*, Vol. 1, No. 3, July 1951.
"James Joyce: Trivial and Quadrivial." *Thought*, Vol. 28, Spring, 1953.
Preface to H. A. Innis, *The Bias of Communication*. Toronto: University of Toronto Press, 1964.

Some Books on McLuhan

Rosenthal, Raymond, ed. *McLuhan Pro and Con*. New York: Funk & Wagnalls, 1968.
Stearn, Gerald Emanuel, ed. *McLuhan Hot and Cool*. New York: Dial, 1967.

INDEX